OMINOU'

Grant Stevens
and
Team Alpha Tango

by

Jamie Fredric

Other Books by Jamie Fredric:

Mission Critical
Black Ops 1

Warning Order
Black Ops 2

In the Mouth of the Wolf
Black Ops 3

Sacrifice of One
Black Ops 4

Last Op
Black Ops 5

Shanghai Mission (#6)

Code Name Antares (#7)

Operation Gold Eagle (#8)

Silent Vengeance (#9)

The Bratva Heist (#10)

Operation Eagle Strike (#11)

Visit: jfredric.blogspot.com

Dedication

For All Those Who Have Served

*

All Gave Some, Some Gave All

*

To: "Witchdoctor 7" - Welcome Home!

THE FREEDOM OF MANY

IS PROTECTED BY THE FEW

Team Alpha Tango
Home Base - "Eagle 8"

Grant Stevens - Captain, (Ret.); graduate U.S. Naval Academy; born in California; brown hair; brown eyes, 6'1"; fluent in Russian and Japanese; Code name "Panther"; Team call sign: "Yankee Zero-Niner"

Joe Adler - Lieutenant, (Ret.); born in Oklahoma; brown hair, blue eyes, 5'10"; fluent in German; Code name "Mustang"; "Yankee Two-Seven"

Vince Milone - Petty Officer 1st Class; born in NJ; brown hair, brown eyes, 5'10"; SB rate (Special Warfare Boat Operator); fluent in Italian, German; "Yankee Three-Six"

Ken Slade - CPOS (Senior Chief), (Ret.); born in Alaska; bald; brown eyes; 5'10"; pointman/navigator; speaks the Inuit language, and Russian; "Yankee Four-One"

Cal "Doc" Stalley - Petty Officer 1st Class; born in Virginia; dark blond hair; blue eyes; 5'10"; corpsman; fluent in French, some Chinese; "Yankee Five-Two"

Darius "DJ" James - Petty Officer 1st Class; born in Florida; dark brown hair; brown eyes; 5'9"; communications; speaks Turkish, Arabic/Farsi; "Yankee Six-Eight"

Mike Novak - Petty Officer 1st Class; born in Wisconsin; dark blond hair; hazel eyes; 6'0"; sniper; speaks Hungarian and some German; "Yankee Seven-Three"

Matt Garrett - Captain, (Ret.); graduate U.S. Naval Academy; born in Maryland; brown hair; brown eyes, 6'0"; fluent in French and German; "Yankee Eight-Four"

Rob Draper - Lieutenant; OCS, Newport, R.I.; born in Connecticut; brown hair; hazel eyes; 5'9"; fluent in French; "Yankee Niner-Niner"

Nick Kalinin (a.k.a. Kyle A. Nichols) - Former KGB agent; born in Kursk, Russia; brown hair; brown eyes; 6'2"; graduate, University of Virginia; fluent in Russian, English, some German; "Yankee Niner-Five"

Chapter 1

Buenaventura, Colombia
Friday
0605 Hours

Typical early morning fog began dissipating along the coast, slowly giving way as the ambient temperature increased to 79°. By sunset the heat with the combined humidity would be an oppressive 91°.

Container and cargo ships that were either heading to or coming from the Panama Canal traveled the ten miles along Buenaventura Bay, eventually reaching the docks of the main port of Colombia on the Pacific coast.

Just after daybreak, when peddlers along the docks began setting up their stands, a young teenage boy rode his beat-up bike away from the slums, briefly escaping the violence and gunfire that pervaded his neighborhood.

The past two mornings of his five-day routine failed to provide what he was looking for, but he continued following orders, and would until his task was completed. This might be his only opportunity to help ensure he and his family had some semblance of protection from the violence. A man he only knew as Rafael, a member of a major guerrilla organization in Colombia, had offered him that chance.

On this third morning he rode once again to the designated location. Across the street from an entrance to the docks was a decrepit shack, covered partly by a slanted tin roof. Running a hand under the back section, he was surprised but relieved at finding the small black case exactly where it was supposed to be. He tucked it under his T-shirt, then peddled away at full speed.

What is in it? he wondered, until in his mind he heard Rafael's raspy voice issuing the warning: "Do not open the case." Without looking back, he rode to a bar in the center of the city, just as he had the past two days. He leaned his bike against the wall, then knocked on the side door. His instructions were to give a report to anyone who answered, unless he had found the case. But he was taken aback when Rafael opened the door, not realizing he'd been seen approaching from the front window. He removed the case from under his shirt and handed it to Rafael, who, without a word, immediately closed the door.

He walked his bike from the alley, then started his twenty-minute ride home. He was ten minutes from the slums when a shot rang out. The violent impact of the round against his lanky body knocked him off his bike.

Citizens in the area scrambled for cover. Doors slammed shut. No one came to help, leaving him lying in his own blood, as the last breath left his young body.

*

In a dingy back room of the bar, Rafael ordered his men to leave. He placed the case on a rickety wooden table centered under a hanging light bulb. Inside the case was a white, sealed envelope containing a single sheet of paper with one word printed in black ink: "RIGHT-EOUS."

He dropped the case into a rusted bucket. Placing the paper back in the envelope, he struck a match, then set the envelope on fire. With only a corner of the envelope remaining, he dropped it into the bucket, as black, disintegrating remnants floated into the air.

The same one-word message, with one meaning, whether on paper or word of mouth, was being secretly passed to guerrilla groups stationed around Colombia. There was only one meaning for this particular code word, the person they'd been expecting was finally in-country: Shahbaz, the Iranian, was ready to lead them.

Chapter 2

Valle del Cauca, Colombia

Work in an illegal gold mine had proceeded for over five years. Fearing that the use of any type of heavy mining machinery would have drawn unwanted attention, miners carved out the main tunnel using only manual labor. They dug through rocks and dirt, survived three cave-ins, when it was finally decided to end the operation. All their work produced little of the precious metal. They moved their illegal operation one hundred miles north.

The citizens of a nearby village discovered the mine three years ago. Instead of continuing to follow the main tunnel, they started digging another, almost parallel to the original. Again, the work was done using manual labor. Hand-held bellows were used to constantly refresh the air. The slow process for carving out the narrow tunnel seemed endless. Little by little the precious metal was exhumed. It was barely enough to change their way of life and their meager existence, but they persisted.

Flowing from a mountain miles away, a wide, fast-moving river narrowed to a mere few feet as it reached the base of the hill. The clear, cool water snaked its way around and over rocks and fallen branches, then continued flowing past the village, supplying its citizens with water for their daily lives.

But everything changed when a group of foreigners assumed control of the mine, recruiting them to continue digging the new tunnel. The original tunnel's vertical depth and distance inward from its entrance was more than enough to satisfy the foreigners for their future needs.

The villagers were ordered to never enter the original tunnel. To ensure they followed the order, one or two guards would be posted 24/7. Fear prevented the villagers from asking questions, even after being told they would no longer have rights to any found gold. Instead, they would earn wages that were less than meager. If a family worked together, as most did, only the head of the household received compensation.

While a majority of the village men actually worked the mine, women and children carried rocks in canvas sacks down to the river. But a new procedure and element had been introduced. Mercury. The amalgam was burned off over an open flame, separating the mercury from the gold. The excess element drained directly into the once pristine water. None of them had any idea that the mercury they were ordered to use would turn their drinking water toxic.

Although they never questioned, the villagers suspected unusual deliveries were being made to the mine during evening hours. When they reported to work in the morning, guards ensured they never strayed into the original tunnel. They only worked from sunrise to sunset because any lights, both inside and out, were strictly prohibited. Any use of machinery could endanger the entire operation.

They were constantly monitored, especially when leaving in the evening. Once they departed, at least two guards remained on duty, armed with AK-47s and

Browning 9mm, semi-automatic pistols.

In addition to the gold, the guards were protecting a cache of weapons: RPG launchers and grenades; 9K32 *Strela-2s*, (NATO name SA-7 *Grail)* shoulder-fired, low-altitude SAMs with high explosive warhead and passive infrared homing guidance; AK-47s; H.E. grenades; ammo. After being shipped from Cuba everything was transported from Venezuela using older Russian Ural-4320s, general purpose off-road 6x6 vehicles. Well aware of spy satellites, the trucks were only driven at night, and off major roads.

Usually, every month a new five-man team would arrive from Venezuela, relieving the team stationed at the village, their base of operations, one half mile from the mine.

But this month was different when an additional five men arrived. The current assignment for these five members of Iran's Quds Force had nothing to do with mine security.

*

Saturday
9 March
0330 Hours

Driving with only parking lights, the driver guided the four-wheel drive vehicle along the dirt road, steering it deeper into the jungle, until reaching a T in the road, where another more narrow dirt road crossed. He backed up twenty yards, ensuring the vehicle was completely hidden from view, then shut off the engine.

With NVGs down and locked, five men, wearing dark green cammies, exited, then slung nylon web rifle straps over their heads. Their AK-47s, with forty-round box magazines, and set to semi-automatic, were held across their chests. Side holsters held Browning hi-power, 9mm, single-action, semi-automatic pistols.

The pointman would depend on a compass hanging from a cord around his neck. They had over a half mile walk, all under heavy tree canopy before reaching the target, the only clearing they would come across. He pulled a razor sharp machete from a sheath hanging from his belt, prepared to cut through the jungle.

Bijan Akbari, Kenan Habib, Arash Imani, and Vahid Mazdaki fell in line behind Roshan Jafari.

Chapter 3

Holding up his hand, Jafari brought everyone to a stop, then motioned them closer. He slid the machete into the sheath, then drew his pistol.

Imani raised his NVGs, then looked through NV glasses (binoculars). As expected, no lights shown from inside the abandoned home. No vehicles were in sight. They had enough time to do a recon of the entire property, then establish offensive and defensive positions.

Just as daylight was breaking, they rushed across open ground, heading for the house. Four of them immediately spread out, beginning a recon, while Imani stood watch under a tin roof overhang, supported on both sides by thick-cut timbers. He backed up against the wooden door, and reaching behind him, he turned the doorknob, but the latch refused to budge. He faced the door and tried again, giving the knob a forceful turn. The latch unlocked. Relieved, he began keeping eyes on the property and road leading from it.

Five minutes later Jafari came around from the north side. "There are tire tracks only on that side but they have been there awhile."

"Can you tell how many vehicles?"

"Only one."

"Stand watch while I look inside." Imani entered cautiously, his sense of smell immediately detecting a strong, musty odor. He removed a flashlight from his pants pocket. Even in daylight the interior remained dark. He shined the light around one large open room. Windows were closed, but all were intact. Simple wood chairs were shoved haphazardly around a wood table at the rear of the room. *Primitive,* he scoffed. He walked toward a partially open door. Kicking it fully open, he aimed the light around the bedroom, seeing two cots, and one single bed, with a boxspring, but no mattress.

Closing the door until it was the way he found it, he then returned to the middle of the main room, trying to decide where to set up positions. Very few places inside would give them sufficient cover. His eyes went to each of the closed windows. *It will not work,* he thought, *not during daylight.* He went outside and met the rest of the team. Their alternatives were few for setting the ambush, protecting each other, and ensuring . . .

"We need to decide," Jafari said glancing at his watch.

Akbari pointed to the roof. "Vahid and I can take positions up there, one on either side. The pitch of the roof should give us enough cover."

Imani said, "No. Only you. Vahid, you take a position inside the tree line on the south side. Kenan, Roshan, and I will spread out along the north side where a vehicle was previously parked. Everyone, take your positions. Stay alert and remember the plan."

Chapter 4

Buenaventura, Colombia
Saturday
9 March
0545 Hours

Not far from Buenaventura's transportation terminal,
along Calle 9, the roof of a five-story building offered a
view of the bay and its estuaries.

Two men, clean shaven, and dressed in black T-shirts
and black pants, carried *Desert Eagles* in side holsters.
The semi-automatic pistols used gas-operated mechanisms normally found in rifles. Magazines were fully
loaded with eight, .44 Magnum rounds. Hanging from
one man's shoulder strap was a Mini-Uzi, with an extended forty-round magazine. The other man had a semi-
automatic-only Galil *("Galatz")* sniper rifle, fitted with a
Nimrod scope, and a 25-round box magazine. A multi-
functional muzzle device acted both as a flash suppressor
and a muzzle brake.

Staying well behind the roof parapet, walking in opposite directions, they moved quietly. Every so often
they'd duck low, then move closer to the parapet. Taking
a knee, they'd scan the docks and parking lots using their
high-power glasses. If anything or anyone caught their
attention, they'd quickly zero in using the rifle scope.

At 0300, they had received new intel that had few
changes since yesterday's report. David Rabin checked
his watch, then whispered into his mic, notifying Ben
Malachi that they had fifteen more minutes of sur-

veillance. At 0600 they'd meet the other two team members waiting at the hotel, then head to their objective fifteen miles west of Buenaventura. Normal driving time was less than half an hour, but traffic through town was always absurd. And even when they reached the outskirts, road construction along the entire route could mean further delays. But they were allowing themselves more than enough time to secure the objective's perimeter, then wait for their contacts, who were scheduled to arrive around 0800.

At 0550 Rabin punched numbers into the secure sat phone. "All clear. On our way to you in five. Copy?"

"Copy," Moshe Agassi, replied. "Vehicle is ready for departure. Out." He laid the phone on the side table, then stood. "They're leaving in five," he said to Ashira Neman.

"Good," Neman said. She rolled up the sleeves of her dark, green shirt, before tightening the rubber band securing her long, braided brown hair. "I'm eager to get on the road." She folded the stock of a Mini-Uzi, and stashed it in a plain, canvas shoulder bag. The last thing she did was to feed a black web belt through the loops of her black jeans, then through the holster. Her Glock was loaded, already in the canvas bag. That's where it would remain until they were underway.

At 0615, an older, faded green Renault commercial panel van, driven by Agassi, was on its way out of the city. In about two and a half hours the four Israelis, all former members of the IDF (Israel Defense Forces), and now Mossad, would meet their American contacts.

Chapter 5

Saturday
0700 Hours

As the house came into view, Agassi downshifted, then kept the vehicle at a steady, slow speed. Using glasses, Rabin, Malachi, and Neman each scanned a section of the property and surrounding jungle, looking for signs that unknown vehicles had possibly trespassed.

"So far, so good," Rabin announced.

Agassi parked on the north side of the house. The four exited then went to the rear of the van. Agassi opened the door. Neman dragged her canvas bag across the floorboards, removed the Mini-Uzi, and unfolded its stock. Carrying the bag and weapon, she headed for the house, wrinkling her nose. "I expect the smell inside has not improved."

"Then open the windows," Rabin told her. He and the two men turned away, rested their hands on their pistols, then kept eyes on the surrounding area.

This mission wasn't the first time Neman was the first in, and it wouldn't be the last. Most of the time was voluntary. She went through the same rigorous training as her male counterparts, and had been with the IDF for four years before being interviewed then selected to become Mossad. She proved herself time and again. This time the likelihood of anyone being inside was highly unlikely. But still . . .

She put the canvas bag just outside the door, then with her weapon ready, she opened the door wide, then took cautious steps into the house. The main room seemed to be the same as they left it. She set her eyes on the bedroom. With the barrel of the weapon, she slowly pushed the door back until it struck the wall. Aiming the weapon straight ahead, she entered, allowing her eyes and weapon to slowly sweep the entire room, looking into shadows, around the beds. She backed out, went to the front door, and shouted, "Clear!" She hurriedly grabbed the canvas bag and put it on the table, before rushing back to the doorway with her Mini-Uzi trained on the front property.

Rabin waved, then gave instructions to Agassi and Malachi, each to inspect a particular side of the property, while he handled the property leading toward the road. With pistols in one hand, and glasses in the other, the men began their assignments. They had about forty-five minutes before the Americans were scheduled to arrive.

The cursory inspection took little time before Malachi and Agassi rounded the corner of the house, meeting Rabin by the van, who was about to remove his sniper rifle from the floorboard.

Suddenly, an explosion of sound caught them off guard. Coming out of nowhere, the semi-automatic weapons fired non-stop. Neman dropped to a knee, aimed the Uzi and fired consecutive bursts.

Within milliseconds of the first sounds, window glass shattered. Neman crawled inside taking cover behind the open door.

AK-47 rounds penetrated Malachi's chest, broke bones in his leg. Blood spurted from arteries.

Rabin had no time to adjust his sniper rifle, but instinctively pulled his pistol from the holster. He was firing and scooting backwards, attempting to take cover behind the van, when rounds penetrated his shoulder and abdomen. Losing his balance he started turning when another round pierced his side, breaking ribs, puncturing his lungs.

Agassi was on his belly, firing his Mini-Uzi from alongside the van. He aimed toward the muzzle flashes coming from his eleven o'clock, flashes that never ceased. He was nearly out of ammo. All he had left was his pistol with eight rounds. There was no way in hell he could reach the extras in the van, or the weapons his dead or dying teammates still had grasped in their hands. He suddenly realized he no longer heard a sound coming from the house, from Neman's weapon. If he could make it to the house, he might have a chance, a chance to stay alive until the Americans arrived. Taking a breath, he fired off a round, then began crabbing his way backwards. Rounds from the aggressors continued striking the van, skidding across the ground, kicking up dirt around him. Keeping his head down, he kept moving, until rounds from an AK-47 slammed in between his shoulder blades and lower back, severing the aorta.

On the house roof, Akbari raised his head, then waved his weapon side to side, signaling his teammates that it was over.

Imani, Habib, Mazdaki and Jafari slung the rifle straps over their heads, as they came running from their cover, with Jafari shouting, "We must hurry! Hide the bodies and weapons in the van."

"But the blood!" Mazdaki said, pointing to the

ground.

"Kick some dirt over it. Hurry!" Jafari drew his Browning pistol as he ran to the house, then stood in the doorway, eyeing empty bullet casings around his feet, and then the damage inside. Shattered window glass was strewn around the room. His eyes briefly settled on a canvas bag on a table, before focusing on the partly open bedroom door.

Holding his pistol steady, while staying back and to the side of doorway, he called out in English, "It is over! They are all dead! You must show yourself—now!"

Ashira Neman stood up from behind the bed, then slowly walked toward the Iranian.

Chapter 6

Palmira, Colombia
Saturday
0605 Hours

A Gulfstream IV, tail number N7325E, registered to a private company in the U.S., landed on Runway 20 at Alfonso Bonilla Aragón International Airport. With navigation lights flashing, it taxied toward a designated space near the terminal.

Two crewmen and four passengers had their phony passports ready to show customs officials. While the crew began its post-flight checklist, the passengers ensured all professional gear was hidden. However, four overnight bags holding civilian clothes remained in plain sight, even if only for appearance sake.

Once the customs officials departed, the plane's exit door was closed, and window shades lowered. The four men began readying themselves to continue on to their destination. Already dressed in black pants, with black T-shirts covering bullet-resistant vests, they secured their Glocks in side holsters. Leather satchels held Uzis with folding stocks, along with extra magazines with .45 ACP rounds and extra mags for Glocks. T-shirts were pulled low, ensuring holsters were concealed.

As a safety net, two of them each carried a GPS, programmed with the coordinates of their destination, agreed upon by the upcoming meeting's participants. According to their contacts, once they left the highway, a heavy tree canopy would allow only limited use of a

GPS.

Aside from examining detailed maps and reviewing intel, the territory they were heading to was unknown. Previous trips had been to Cartagena and Bogotá. Those cities, including Cali, were plagued by armed conflict, drug trafficking, violence, and the presence of guerrilla and paramilitary groups.

The four picked up their gear, then stopped near the exit door. Gary Nyland and Chuck Sands, pilots, shook hands with each of them, wishing them good luck. Nyland added, "We'll contact D.C. about our arrival, then again when you advise you've made contact with the Israelis."

Once the men left the aircraft, the door was closed then Nyland and Sands, both special agents with CIA's Special Activities Air Group, went aft. Sands started a fresh pot of coffee. Nyland took out two chicken salad sandwiches from the fridge, then glanced at his watch. "We should hear from them in a couple of hours. That's more than enough time for them to reach the objective."

*

A rented four-wheel drive Nissan Patrol departed the airport and headed north toward the town of Buga, with a final destination west of it.

Clint Beatty, Pete Kaufman, Joel Salzman, and Sam Jacobs were well aware of the risk they were taking in this current assignment, but it wasn't any different from past missions. All were part of the CIA's Special Operations Group, and understood that if they were captured or compromised, their government could, and most likely would deny any knowledge.

Well past the airport, the driver, Kaufman, increased speed. Beatty, Jacobs, and Salzman removed their high-power glasses from cases. Beatty, in the front passenger seat, and Salzman each held a GPS. Kaufman's Glock and glasses were on the console.

*

"We're approaching coordinates for the turnoff," Beatty said, then pointed, "It's just ahead on the left." Kaufman slowed the vehicle, then pulled onto the right shoulder, stopping opposite the one-lane dirt road that was almost unnoticeable. According to intel and sat images, the two-mile route to the target had been cut through the jungle. Tree limbs and palm fronds intermittently draped over the road, temporarily shielding it from the hot sun.

Kaufman engaged the four-wheel drive, preparing for the dirt road, and for crossing the river. Its depth was no more than eight inches, its distance to the opposite side about thirty yards, but both banks were slick, muddy, and the riverbed was covered with stones and small rocks.

"All clear this way," Jacobs said, keeping watch out the rear window.

Kaufman turned across the highway, then proceeded down a slight incline, briefly stopping at the water's edge. Easing the vehicle into the water, he felt the steering wheel shimmy as tires navigated over varying sized slick rocks.

The vehicle's angle slowly changed as Kaufman guided it up the bank, its tires negotiating the soft mud. At the top of the bank, and even though the vehicle was on solid ground, he left the four-wheel drive engaged. The decision to drive the vehicle directly to the target was made early on as a just in case—just in case the mission turned into one big clusterfuck, and when hauling ass might be the only realistic option.

Call signs, radio, and sat phone frequencies had been set. But it had been agreed upon by both parties that there'd be no communication between them once the operation was fully underway and only when the Americans were close to the target. Experience dictated to proceed with caution, even though the Israelis were expected to be on-site.

Once the vehicle was on level ground, Kaufman shifted into neutral then set the parking brake. The men took Uzis from satchels, then slammed in magazines. They drew their Glocks from holsters, and screwed on suppressors. All side windows were lowered. Jacobs kept his focus out the rear window. Using his glasses, Salzman paid attention to both sides. Beatty and Kaufman focused on the road and dense jungle ahead.

Kaufman whispered, "Let's roll."

*

They'd traveled nearly two miles when Kaufman stopped the vehicle clear of any tree canopy where the GPS wouldn't be obstructed. "Distance to coordinates?"

Salzman and Beatty each checked a GPS, with Beatty

replying, "Seventy-five yards, slightly left." Aside from the coordinates, all they had to go on was the sat image that showed the target, and except for the cleared grounds encircling the house, it was surrounded entirely by jungle. The only other homes, both abandoned, were located at least a mile away, both south of the target, on the side of rolling hills.

Kaufman downshifted, slowly bringing the vehicle to a slow stop before he shifted into neutral. Earpieces and throat mics were adjusted, tested. Kaufman laid his Glock in his lap. Watches were synchronized. Preparing for Beatty to make contact, windows were rolled up.

With the radio in his left hand, and his Glock on the dash within easy reach, Beatty asked quietly, "Ready?"

"Go," came three whispered responses.

Beatty pressed the button, and speaking softly, said, "Desert Leopard, Desert Leopard, this is Badger Four. Do you copy? Over." Silence. He repeated, "Desert Leopard, this is Badger Four. Do . . you . . copy? Over.

A female finally answered, "Badger Four, this is Desert Leopard. Over."

"Desert Leopard, we are on access road, stopped about seventy-five yards from you. Confirm it's clear to proceed. Over."

"Confirming . . clear. Over."

"Roger. Proceeding now. Out."

Salzman leaned toward the front seats. "Listen, why don't Sam and I follow on foot, just as a precaution."

With everyone in agreement, Salzman and Jacobs got out, then quietly shut the doors. Sliding the Glocks into the holsters, they hooked the straps holding the Uzis over their shoulders, raised the weapons, then rested index fingers outside the trigger guards. Looking into the vehicle, Salzman saw Kaufman's eyes in the rearview mirror and gave him a thumb's up.

Kaufman shifted into gear, and eased the vehicle forward. Salzman and Jacobs stayed closed, occasionally walking backwards, quickly looking in every direction, hearing nothing but chirping birds, rustling of leaves and palms fronds, normal jungle sounds.

Kaufman spoke into his mic, notifying Salzman and Jacobs the objective was in sight, and that he was braking. The two stepped next to the rear side doors, opened them, then continued on watch near those open doors.

Beatty focused his glasses. "There's the green van." He zeroed in on the house open front door, seeing a woman step into the doorway, and holding a radio. She waved a hand high overhead. "That's her," Beatty confirmed.

"See anybody else?" Kaufman asked, while keeping one hand on the steering wheel and another on the gearshift.

Beatty scanned the entire front of the house, then focused on the door. "There's a man behind her, but I can't get a good look."

"So," Kaufman began, "we're still missing two."

Beatty pressed the transmit button. "Desert Leopard, where are your teammates? Over." He raised his glasses, focusing on her.

She hesitated a brief moment before pointing to each side of the house, and responded, "They are finishing a recon before our meeting begins. Over."

"Understood. Out." Beatty laid the radio on the console, then called over his shoulder, "Sam, Joel, get in. Okay, Pete, let's go."

Chapter 7

Kaufman drove toward the parked van, then made a wide U-turn, stopping in front of the house, facing the road. Doors opened immediately when Kaufman shut down the engine. The men exited carrying their Uzis. Kaufman and Salzman met up with their teammates on the other side of the vehicle.

"Where'd she go?" Kaufman questioned, no longer seeing Neman in the doorway.

An odd sound on the roof distracted the men's attention just long enough before they heard multiple voices, coming from different directions, shouting orders in English, "Drop your weapons! Drop your weapons!"

"What the fuck?!" Kaufman roared.

Kneeling near the edge of the roof, Akbari fired his weapon, intentionally aiming at the vehicle. The AK-47 round shattered the rear window, penetrated seats, slammed into the dashboard.

Imani stood in the open doorway, aiming his weapon, and ordering, "Drop your weapons, unless you want to die right now!"

"Christ!" Beatty swore.

The four men slowly laid down their Uzis, then heard, "Now, get rid of those sidearms!" Four Glocks hit the ground. Imani shouted, "On your knees! Hands behind your heads!"

Only after the Americans complied did they see men rushing toward them, from the south side and from behind the cover of trees at the edge of the clearing. After they were in position, Akbari lowered himself from the roof, then stood near his teammates.

Imani walked behind each man, then yanked each throat mic, snapping the wire leading to the PTT assembly.

Even though their English was perfect, their mustaches and short full beards, dark green cammies, berets and AK-47s confirmed for the SOG team who they were.

"Iranians," Beatty whispered out of the side of his mouth.

Within the blink of an eye, Imani was behind him, striking his skull with the rifle butt. Unconscious, Beatty collapsed next to Jacobs.

"You sonofabitch!" Jacobs bellowed, reaching to help Beatty.

Habib swung his rifle, the front sight and barrel making contact just under Jacobs' cheekbone. The force of the impact knocked him sideways, made him lightheaded. Blood spilled from a deep, wide gash, flowed down his cheek, and trickled into his mouth. He gingerly pressed a hand against the wound, feeling warm blood oozing under his fingers, tasting it in his mouth.

With just that brief moment of distraction, Kaufman saw his chance, and dove forward, reaching for Jafari's legs. A rifle sound cracked the air. The 7.62×39mm round, fired from Imani's weapon, blew a hole through Kaufman's vest, then his body. He was dead within seconds.

Imani pointed toward the agents, then speaking in Farsi, he said to his men, "Get them ready to leave. We will drive their vehicle. It will take less time than walking them through the jungle."

"What about him?" Mazdaki asked using his rifle to

point at Kaufman's body.

"Once we are ready to go, put him in the house."

Salzman was the only one whose mind was still functioning clearly, and more than enough to understand Farsi. *Where the fuck are they taking us?* A picture of the Mossad woman, standing in the doorway, flashed through his mind. *And what the fuck happened to her and the other Israelis?*

His eyes first went to Beatty, who was on his knees, trying to maintain his balance, blinking his eyes constantly, attempting to focus, and probably having one bitchin' headache. Jacobs was pressing a bloody hand against the oozing wound.

Finally, Salzman looked at Kaufman's body. There wasn't anything he could do for him, and that turned his stomach, more so than knowing his government would deny any knowledge of he and his teammates. But since they never confirmed with the pilots that contact had been made with the Israelis, Nyland and Sands would notify Langley. Even so, would it matter?

His thoughts were distracted when Akbari stepped closer to them, while the other three Iranians began tying their hands behind their backs, blindfolding them with strips of torn, white cloth, then finally jerking them to their feet. Waiting for the Iranians' next move, Salzman tried concentrating on the sounds around him.

The first voice he heard was Akbari questioning: "What is taking so long?"

What's he waiting for? Salzman silently questioned. *Are there others inside?* An instant picture went through his mind of the woman being treated the same as them, blindfolded, tied up, or worse. He turned his head toward the sound of footsteps.

"Put them in their vehicle," Imani ordered, as he led Ashira Neman from the house. First, he pointed toward Akbari. "You drive." Then pointing to himself and Jafari he said, "We will go with you. The rest of you head to our vehicle. We will meet as planned." Habib and Mazdaki ran toward the trail.

Chapter 8

Washington, D.C.
Saturday
1045 Hours - Local Time

Grant reached for Claudia Stockwell's hand as they walked from the lobby of her apartment building and into a cool fifty-three degrees. "You look terrific. You know that little black dress is absolutely my favorite. Too bad you had to cover it with a coat," he commented with a wide smile.

"Yes, I know. You're looking pretty sharp yourself."

"You mean, for a change?" he laughed.

"You always look good," she replied squeezing his hand.

Grant opened the Vette's passenger side door, then held her hand while she got in. Her coat flopped open. He couldn't help noticing her dress sliding higher up her thighs. She wriggled in the seat, pulling it down, while coyly looking up at him.

"Like I said," he winked, "that dress is my favorite." He closed the door then went around to the driver's side, tossed his overnight bag into the back, then settled into the bucket seat and started the engine. The 454 big block roared to life. Just then one of his weird feelings shot through him. All he could do was ignore it and hope nothing would interrupt the planned evening.

"Grant, is anything wrong?" she asked, laying a hand on his arm.

"What? Oh, nothing. Okay, here's the plan. Brunch first, show second, and for the finale, a dinner cruise on the Potomac. Sound good?"

"Oh, most definitely!" She watched him for a moment before asking, "Do you still miss it, Grant?"

"What?"

"The Navy, being on ships?"

"I guess certain aspects of it, except those reasons might be hard to explain. But, yeah, every now and then I still have my moments."

Shifting into gear, he eased the Vette toward the exit, then pulled into traffic. Ten minutes later the phone rang. As he reached for it, he noticed her watching him, her smile disappearing. *She's already expecting a change in plans,* he thought.

"Stevens."

"Skipper, it's me. We have a situation."

Oh shit! he silently swore, remembering the weird feeling. "Hold on a minute while I pull over." Once alongside the curb, he shifted the phone to his left hand, then reached for hers, giving it a light squeeze. She looked away.

"Okay. Talk to me."

"First confirm that Claudia's with you."

"Affirm."

"I'll be brief." Since Grant's phone wasn't secure, Adler realized he had to keep specifics to a minimum. "I just got a call. You've received an invite to the 'House.'"

"That's it? No other details?"

"Only a destination. I'm to confirm that I relayed the message to you. I've already contacted the guys to cancel their plans. They're on their way to Eagle 8. I know you can't talk right now, but do you want me to contact Scott to see if he's gonna be involved?"

"Better hold off for now. Make your call, then give me an update in about ten minutes."

"Don't break the speed limit." Adler hung up, then thought about Grant having to tell Claudia. "Wouldn't wanna be in his shoes right about now," he said under his breath.

Grant laid down the phone. "I'm sorry, Claudia."

"You don't have to explain. Just take me home."

He shifted into gear, checked traffic in both directions, then made a U-turn. They were both quiet during the short drive. He pulled into the apartment complex parking lot, then immediately shut off the engine. Before she could object, he was hurrying to the passenger side. He opened the door, and offered his hand. "C'mon. I'll walk you to the lobby."

"That's all right. You don't have time."

Ouch, he thought. "C'mon."

When they were close to the entrance she released his hand, looked up into his brown eyes, then placed a hand against his chest. "Take care of yourself."

He drew her close, gently wrapped his strong arms around her, then he kissed her. She returned his kiss, lingering briefly, feeling the warmth of his body against hers, but then, abruptly, she turned away and walked into the lobby without looking back.

He kept his eyes on her as she waited near the elevator. He suspected she was questioning their relationship—again. *End of story? Maybe this isn't the right time, but . . .* He hurried into the lobby just as she stepped into the elevator. As the door started closing he pressed his arm against it, forcing it open. He kept his voice low, while looking to into her eyes. "This is my life, Claudia. You know that."

"Yes, I know, and I also know what happened to you on some of your missions." Tears welled up in her hazel eyes, her voice cracked. "I don't understand how you . . ."

They both went quiet, until Grant said, "I can't apologize for who I am, Claudia." He hesitated before adding, "Look, we can talk when I get back, unless you'd . . . unless you'd rather not. Just tell me yes or no."

She wiped a tear from her cheek. "Call me when you're back home, so I know you're okay."

"Sure. Sure I will." He stood by the elevator waiting until the doors closed. Lowering his head for a moment, he turned and walked from the lobby while thinking, *It's not the first time a relationship's gone south because of my work.* "Dammit!" he quietly mumbled through gritted teeth. He gave the exit door a hard shove, then immediately broke into a jog.

No sooner had he settled in the bucket seat, when the phone on the console rang. His irritation was obvious as he answered, "Stevens!"

"Whoa! What the hell's wrong . . .? Oh, wait. You and Claudia . . .?"

"Later. What's happening, Joe?"

"Where you at?"

"In the apartment parking lot." He started the engine, shifted into first, then drove toward the exit. "Got an update?"

"Go to the usual parking area, then the normal entrance. Someone will greet you there."

"Okay, Joe. Listen, research as much as you can on the destination."

"And I'll have the guys start readying gear necessary for the environment."

"Thanks. Talk to you later." He laid down the phone, then pulled onto the side street. Tires squealed as he stomped on the gas.

Chapter 9

White House
Saturday
1115 Hours

Rushing down the hallway, red-haired Chief of Staff Jeff Muncie offered a hand as he greeted Grant. "Captain Stevens, I'm Jeff Muncie. It's been a while since we met, but it never seems to be under the best of circumstances, I'm afraid."

"Unfortunately, you're right, sir."

"Come with me."

Grant followed Muncie down the hallway, expecting the meeting to be in the "Cement Mixer," the Secret Service code name for the Situation Room. He heard voices coming from behind the closed door, but to his surprise, Muncie led him past the room, then up the stairs, eventually ending up in the Oval Office.

"Mr. President, Captain Stevens is here," Muncie announced.

Carr was standing behind his desk by the large windows, rolling up the sleeves of his white shirt. He waved Grant in, then walked toward him, offering a hand. "Grant, how are you?"

"I'm good, sir."

Carr motioned to Muncie. "Okay, Jeff. That'll be all."

Once Muncie left, Carr noticed Grant's gray sports jacket, white shirt, black pants, which suggested he may have had personal plans. "Did we interrupt your evening,

Grant?"

"Not a problem, sir."

"Hmm. I have a feeling that's not the case. Well, I'm sorry." Carr pointed toward a hallway. "Come with me to the library. As they walked, Carr asked, "So tell me, how was Luke's graduation ceremony from BUD/S?"

"Amazing, sir. Walking onto the compound, the grinder brought back a lot of memories for all of us, but especially seeing those young men receive the Trident."

"And you pinned on Luke's?"

"It was an extraordinary moment. Although, I've gotta admit it's hard to believe I've got a son who's a SEAL."

"I'm sure you've got the usual concerns."

Grant shook his head. "Not about his ability, just the idea he'll be doing the same, uh, activities that I've done for years."

"Activities that you've been very highly successful at, Grant. Don't forget that." Without replying, Grant just nodded.

Once inside the small library, Carr sat in one of the upholstered chairs then pointed toward the desk chair. "Have a seat." Grant rolled back the chair, then sat opposite Carr.

The president took a breath, finally saying, "Grant, what I'm about to tell you is classified Top Secret."

"Understood, sir, but will my men be cleared?"

"You all have Top Secret White House clearances, so you can bring them in."

"Very well. But what about State? Scott's usually involved when it comes to refueling and clearance at airports."

"That will be discussed later." Carr pressed his palms together, then tapped his fingers lightly against his mouth, while keeping his eyes on Grant. "I'll reiterate again, Grant, this is highly classified."

Grant rested his elbows on his knees, and started squeezing one fist then the other. "I understand."

"Four CIA agents, all from its Special Operations Group, were on assignment in Colombia."

"Excuse me, Mr. President, but before you continue, I have a question."

"Go ahead."

"Those men, with them being members of that group, it usually means if their mission is compromised, if they're captured, they'll be . . ."

"Disavowed?"

"Yes, sir."

Carr was quiet for a brief moment, while watching Grant's expression, understanding its meaning. "Grant, you know that's the way it's been since your Team was formed. But you have my word there's no way in hell I wouldn't do everything in my power to see that didn't happen to you, your men, or the others. Understood?"

"Yes, sir."

"All right. Now, let's continue. The agents were to meet with members of Mossad."

Grant sat up straighter. "Most of us who've been in the intel community know there's been cooperation between us, and right here in the U.S., specifically pertaining to Hezbollah. Is that what . . .?"

"It's not about Hezbollah. It's about the Quds Force. Do you know anything about it?"

"Not much, only that it's Iranian, a unit of the Islamic Revolutionary Guard Corps, and it's completely controlled by the military hierarchy of the IRGC."

"That's right. It set up one of its headquarters in the former compound of our Tehran embassy that was overrun back in '79."

"How convenient," Grant mumbled.

"One of its responsibilities is to send foreign recruits to Iran where they're given paramilitary training, then transported back to their home countries. But the Quds Force has taken more than a direct role in the military operations of those trained forces by also providing preattack planning and other operation-specific military advice. In Colombia, those new forces operate in many of the major cities, including Buenaventura."

Grant's brow wrinkled. "Is that where the mission is? Buenaventura?"

"The meeting was taking place about fifteen miles east. You'll learn more in a while. Now, you've probably seen or read reports that Hezbollah has one of the best counterintelligence units in the world. But what you may not know is its counterintelligence was initially managed by the Quds Force."

The right side of Grant's mouth curved up slightly. "So Hezbollah has become number one and the Quds Force has slipped into the number two slot?"

"Not by much, and that's probably the reason they've had assignments in Venezuela and now Colombia." Before Grant could question further, Carr said, "Look, I only wanted to give you a heads up. Those waiting in the Sit Room will fill you in on the important details, and

much more than I can tell you. Your wait won't be long."
Carr stood.

Grant immediately followed his lead, but then asked,
"Mr. President, what time was their meeting to take
place?"

"Around eight this morning. They were to confirm
with the pilots that they made contact with the Israelis.
They never did. Come on. We're expected downstairs."

Chapter 10

White House
Situation Room

Carr briefly revealed the intel he discussed with Grant to the men sitting around the large, oval, mahogany table. Then he nodded toward Simmons. "Ray, go ahead."

CIA Director Ray Simmons pushed his wire-rimmed glasses back on the bridge of his nose. "Captain, open that folder, and look through the first two groups of photos." As Grant started turning over each black and white photo, Simmons said, "The first four men are our agents. The second group is the Mossad team. All names are on the back. And before you ask, you can share the photos and intel with your men." He gave Grant a moment, and then, "The next picture is of Major General Behnam Khorasani. He's the head of the Quds Force, and reports directly to Iran's Supreme Leader."

Examining the photo of a man perhaps in his late fifties, with salt and pepper hair and beard, Grant said, "His name's familiar."

"It should be. Before he took over the Quds Force he was with Hezbollah. He orchestrated the hijacking of the TWA . . ."

"They tortured and killed the Navy diver," Grant interrupted, gritting his teeth. His quiet tone not only revealed his dismay, but his anger.

"You knew him?"

"No, sir, but I know that his brother was a SEAL."

Grant straightened up in the chair. "Does that bastard, oh, sorry, sir. Does that *gentleman* have anything to do with Colombia?"

With a half smile Simmons replied, "Intel from the Israelis confirmed the bastard won't physically be in Colombia, but it's his operation. He's been held in high regard for many years by Iran's supreme leader."

Grant dropped the photo in the folder, then picked up a paper stamped "Top Secret." He quickly perused the report, noticing the makes and models of two vehicles before his eyes settled on what could only be a code name. "Is there an official name that goes with 'Shahbaz'? Do you know the translation?"

"In Persian it means a fabled bird, bigger than a hawk or falcon. That name's been floating around for several years, but neither we nor the Israelis have been able to identify him. There's high confidence he's a sleeper agent, who's been in Europe and Asia."

FBI Kellerman cut in. "There was a time when we all believed he might have been operating in the U.S."

Grant refocused on Simmons. "Is that why your men went to Colombia, to ID him? I would think there would've been some communication between the Israelis and CIA without your men going. My gut's telling me there has to be more to it."

"You're right, Captain." Simmons pointed toward someone standing by a projector, just before an image appeared on the pull-down screen, an image divided into six sections. Everyone shifted in their chairs, as Simmons began, "Those five men have been ID'd by the Israelis, all are Quds Force currently in Colombia, and just beginning their one-month assignment. You'll find the individual pictures in the back of the folder. We'll get to more later."

Simmons requested the next slide, showing an image of a cargo ship. "That's the Syrian cargo ship, the *Al Sham*. She's a small-size ship that normally operates with a crew of twelve. She departed Syria's port of Latakia, then traveled directly to Havana where she off-loaded part of her cargo, pistachio nuts and cans of olive oil. Her remaining cargo, olive oil and avocados, was destined for Colombia.

"Three days after arriving in Havana, she began her journey to the Panama Canal, with Buenaventura as her final port before heading back home. Her travel through the Canal will take between ten and twelve hours, so unless there's a delay, she's expected to arrive in port in two days, which should be Monday. She's also supposed to be transporting twenty Colombians the Quds trained in Iran."

"Excuse me a minute, sir, but why use a Syrian vessel?"

"Syria has legitimate trade routes and destinations. Iran's more restrictive, mostly trading in Asia and the Med."

"Won't she be boarded for inspection before passing through the Canal?"

"We notified the authorities, but she's carrying legal cargo, and the Colombians are legally aboard, signed on as acting assistant crew, heading back to their home country. Any other questions?"

"You mentioned the Quds' trainees," Grant began,

"but do you know if there are any local guerrilla groups involved in whatever this is? There's gotta be a helluva lot of them already wreaking havoc in the country, or at least prepared to."

"We believe so. The Israelis intercepted a transmission that something might be going down at the port. The Mossad team ran surveillance up until they departed for the meeting, but they came up empty. Understand, Captain, that Buenaventura, especially around the slums, killings, torture, and everything illegal and unimaginable takes place every day. Guerrilla gangs are constantly at war. It's a wicked, sordid place."

"Understood, sir, but it seems there's a helluva lot going on. Is it all interconnected? Or do the players have different objectives?"

"Grant?" Carr said.

"Yes, sir?"

"We know you're ready to get the mission underway, but just be patient. Okay?"

"Yes, sir." As anxious as he was to learn more, Grant settled back in his chair.

Simmons motioned for another slide. "That's the house where the meeting was taking place. According to the Israelis, from its condition it's been abandoned for a very long time. The team made a recon when they first arrived. The coordinates are in the folder."

Grant arched an eyebrow. "Was there any reason why they selected that out-of-the-way site instead of somewhere in the city?"

"It was closer to the airport, but also near the river where samples were to be collected."

"Samples?"

"Yes. That explanation's coming up." He motioned for another slide. "The sat image shows an area less than two miles from the meeting place. It's mostly jungle." Another image slid onto the screen, with a black arrow pointing down. "Same area, just a closer view. What you can't see is the actual entrance to a mine, a gold mine. The coordinates are also in the folder."

Grant rested his arms on the table, while continuing to look at the image. "Who's hiding what in it?"

"Let me first say that we and the NRO (National Reconnaissance Office) have very carefully examined U-2 and sat images and found that they *are* digging for gold, all by manual labor, using men, women and children." Simmons pointed to the screen. "They carry rocks from the cave along that beaten down path to the river. We suspect mercury is being used as an amalgam and is washing downstream."

"Hence, the samples," Grant said.

Murmurs of obvious disgust and concern came from all those present. Simmons looked toward Grant, then reached across the table, handing him a small glass vial. "I'd like you to get that sample, just in case the . . ."

"Understood, sir." Grant slipped the vial into his jacket pocket.

Simmons continued, "Getting back to your question of what's being hidden, we believe there's a cache of weapons the Iranians recently brought in through Venezuela. Since all this came to light, I've had a satellite repositioned. We've seen at least one Ural-4320, not completely hidden, not far from the mine's entrance. It's large enough to transport weapons and humans. We know the Venezuelans have several Urals, so how many are being used by the Iranians is unknown, but images have detected one making its way to and from the mine, although, there doesn't appear to be any set schedule."

"As far as the gold, do you know if they're stashing it in the mine along with the weapons, or moving it some-place else?"

"A Ural was one of the targets the Mossad team was watching for at the docks, but up until they left, none were spotted, and we don't believe they're transporting the gold to Venezuela. That assumption is being based on the fantastic job the folks at the NRO have done, and continue to do. They've examined the U-2 images up close and personal, and compared Ural tire tracks on the dirt road leading to the mine. The depth appears to be deeper when a truck arrives then when it heads back to Venezuela."

"Which could mean weapons and or humans were on-board."

"Exactly. But as far as the gold, we have to assume it's being stashed at the mine."

"Those NRO folks have sharp eyes, sir. We, and you, know what they can discover." Grant's smile was brief before he asked, "Mr. Director, just how long have the Israelis been in-country?"

"A week. They arrived right after their intel inter-cepted transmissions concerning the *Al Sham*."

"I guess it's safe to say they were aware the Quds Force was in-country."

"Up to a point. I ordered the U-2 to fly over the area

a second time. Those images are still be processed and analyzed at the NRO. Also, our satellites were redirected to focus on increased activity from Venezuela into Colombia, especially along routes leading to Buenaventura."

"But does anyone know exactly what the Quds are planning?"

"Unknown, Captain, but since they've already got a foothold in Venezuela, their next logical major move would be Colombia. There are plenty of oil wells in the North, pipelines running South, and there are cities with refineries."

Grant kneaded a fist against his other palm. "All sites that could cause total disruption to the economy, while they profit from mining gold, emeralds, and silver. And I guess we can't forget the cocaine industry."

"That alone is more than enough reason to strengthen their foothold and cause chaos, Captain. The money to be made is remarkable," Simmons commented.

"Sir, haven't there been *any* recent intercepts coming out of Colombia?"

"We and NSA continue to have ears on, and not just on Colombia, but also on Syria and Iran. So far nothing pertaining to the operation has been detected. One of the reasons is the Quds tend to use walkie talkies and couriers when they're on assignments. And by the way, most of them are fluent in English."

Grant's mind raced. What originally appeared to be a SAR mission (Search and Rescue) was suddenly twisting into something more ominous. His eyes went around the table, not sure which person would answer. "Sirs, what about the Mossad team? When was the last time their government heard from them?"

Secretary of State Pierce McKinley responded, "I spoke with Prime Minister Peritz and Mossad Director Chaikin. The team's last communication was around 0600 this morning, just prior to them leaving Buenaventura. Further contact wasn't expected until the team returned to the city. That timeframe was unclear. Director Chaikin and I agreed to contact one another should any updates occur. So far it's been quiet."

"So, if something nefarious happened to our agents, do you suspect the Mossad team suffered the same fate, and at the hands of the Quds?"

"That's almost impossible to answer, Captain," McKinley responded.

"Let me interject something," Simmons said. "We suspect that a fresh team of the Quds Force travels monthly from Venezuela to relieve the men at the mine. It's very possible that any number could've already slipped into Colombia. The men shown in the earlier slide were acting security at the mine."

Grant remained quiet, his expression indicating something was on his mind. Simmons asked, "What are you thinking, Captain?"

"Sir, there has to be another group or team, I mean, it seems unlikely those men at the mine would be assigned double duty, especially if they had orders to protect a cache of weapons, and ensure the mine operation itself proceeded without interruption. Mr. Director, the situation has the potential to escalate into a full-blown crisis in Colombia, and in the Middle East."

"You're absolutely right. Secretary McKinley and Director Chaikin have expressed their concerns to one another. Director Chaikin and the prime minister are aware that we're sending a team to Colombia to investigate."

"But exactly what *is* our mission, sir?"

"Your main mission is to find, or at least find out what happened to our agents, and possibly the Mossad team."

Grant slowly swiveled his chair, as he thought about all possibilities the Iranians might have planned.

"You have more questions?" Simmons asked.

"What? Oh, yes, sir. It hasn't been long enough to hear whether they're actually holding hostages. I know this may be far-fetched, but if they are, do you think the plan may be to send them to the Middle East aboard the *Al Sham?*"

Simmons didn't respond immediately. Carr waited for a moment, then asked, "Ray, what *do* you think?"

"Anything's possible, Mr. President. I doubt we'd get much cooperation from the local authorities to do a search of the ship, though. With the port and city being a hotbed of violence, for all intent and purposes, they've lost control. Our last chance would be as the ship travels back through the Canal. Once it's in international waters, we're out of luck. Of course, if that's what *is* planned, there's bound to be confirmation relayed back to Tehran. Captain, we'll update you as long as we can."

"Of course, sir." Grant rolled his chair away from the table, then stood. "I'd like to take a minute to run this through my mind." Without waiting for anyone's approval, he walked toward the back of the room, then stood near the Watch Room. Folding his arms across his chest, and with his head down, he mentally visualized the mission, the unknown possibilities, the actions he and his men had to be prepared for, requests he would make from the men in this room.

Slowly blowing out a breath, he returned to his chair, sat down, then looked directly at Secretary of the Navy Canon, and then at Secretary of Defense Daniels. "Sirs, can I safely assume that there's a carrier or LHD (Landing Helicopter Dock) in the Pacific Fleet that's within a reasonable distance from Colombia?"

SecNav Canon flipped open a folder. Turning over a paper, he ran a finger down a column. "An LHD, the USS *Roeti Island* might be the closest."

"And would we have choppers at our disposal for extraction or any other . . . emergency?"

Canon glanced at SecDef Daniels who gave a quick nod. "Of course."

"Very good, sir. And as far as setting frequencies and call signs . . ." Grant looked at Secretary of State McKinley. "Sir, will Agent Mullins be available to receive those frequencies and call signs from the LHD? He can pass them to us when he confirms refueling."

"That'll be arranged."

"Mr. Director," Grant said, turning to look at Simmons, "were the agents going to use sat phones to communicate with the men at the airport?"

Simmons nodded. "I'll see that the frequencies are made available to you."

Carr noticed one of the men in the Watch Room was

signaling him. "What is it, Al?"

"Excuse me, Mr. President, but there's a call for Director Simmons from Deputy Director Gordon."

Simmons rolled his chair back. "He might have word from Colombia."

While he waited, Grant mentally reviewed the mission. *No different from any other,* he thought. *Still plenty of unknowns. Will we be confronting the Quds? And how many? Does DJ have to brush up on his Farsi? He might have to use it when overhearing conversations during surveillance. Or, even better, while running a G2.* He realized it wasn't likely the Quds would voluntarily start speaking in English.

Simmons walked to his seat, his expression leaving little doubt what he learned from his deputy director. "The pilots in Colombia still haven't heard from our agents. I told them to remain on station for now. It'll be a wait and see."

"Is it time for me to get underway?" Grant asked, with his impatience front and center.

"One last thing, Captain. I'm expecting new sat and possibly U-2 images at any time. I'll see that they're faxed to you with any pertinent notations, including the frequencies."

"Very well, sir."

Carr rolled his chair back, then stood. "If that's all, gentlemen, we'd better turn Grant loose," he said smiling. Everyone stood, each man gathering papers and folders.

Handshakes and well wishes were extended to Grant, with Carr being the last. "Grant, while I have full confidence in you successfully completing this mission, remember what I told you earlier."

"I will, Mr. President. I'll pass it along to the Team, sir."

As Grant turned to leave, Carr patted his shoulder. "Godspeed, Grant, and to your men."

Chapter 11

Eagle 8
Saturday
1335 Hours

Team A.T. sat around the dining room table, listening to Grant as he conveyed an overview of his meeting. He opened a folder, removed all the photos, then handed them to Adler, sitting to his right. "Names are on the back," Grant said, as Adler began handing off photos, one by one. Grant added, "Ashira Neman is the only woman assigned to that Mossad team." A.T. didn't question Neman's assignment. They were fully aware of Israeli women's capabilities within the IDF and Mossad.

After a brief discussion on the remaining individuals in the photos, Grant said, "We'll have a more thorough Q&A on them and the mission once we're aboard the *Herc.*" He turned toward Adler. "Joe, give me a quick run-through on weapons and gear you've readied."

Adler reported that Slade was taking a machete. Everyone but Novak would carry an MP5, silenced Sig, K-bar, H.E. (high explosive) grenades, flash-bangs, pencil flares, the usual extra ammo and survival kits. Novak opted for one of his older sniper rifles, since there'd be too much tree canopy for the prototype's GPS to function. Bullet-resistant vests were already in the SUV. Stalley packed a camera.

"Sounds good, Joe, but we've gotta ensure everyone's got water before we make our jump. The heat and humidity will be a bitch. Listen, Ken, I want you to carry a

Remington pump."

"Be happy to, boss." The shotgun was capable of firing 15 rounds per minute. Tubular-shaped magazines held seven rounds each.

Grant was thinking ahead and of all offensive/defensive possibilities that could happen. "Everyone takes a smoke grenade."

"Any particular color?" Adler asked.

"Any color but yellow," Grant smiled.

"You got it."

Matt Garrett walked from a back room, holding a sealed plastic bag. "Grant, here's some cash. It should be enough. You can divvy it up on the plane."

"Okay, Matt. Hang onto it for now. Listen, Joe, I'm thinking we need to take small blocks of C-4, timers, and a remote, maybe two."

"Any particular reason?"

"If we don't find the agents or Mossad team at the house, we're gonna find our way to that mine."

"You honestly think the BGs (bad guys) would've taken the hostages there?"

"Anything's possible, Joe."

"But what the hell are your plans for the explosives, especially if hostages and/or civilians *are* there?"

"Gotta be prepared. There's no way to know the size of the mine, so I'll leave the number of timers in your hands. Are frequencies already set?"

"Sure, a good number of them are always ready."

"To tell you the truth, Joe, the mine isn't all that I'm curious about."

"I'm listening."

"It's that cargo ship."

"Just . . . *curious,* you say?"

"Okay. Maybe that's the wrong word. But its arrival in Buenaventura while all the other shit's going on can't be coincidental."

"What's that gut of yours saying? Wait! Is your intent to possibly cause some very major damage to that ship?!"

A brief grin appeared on Grant's face, leaving Adler just shaking his head. Grant called, "Ken, everybody's to bring masks, fins and snorkels."

"Wetsuits?"

"Negative. The water temp's close to eighty degrees this time of year. I'll give details once we're underway." Slade passed the word, then sent Novak and Milone to complete the task.

Just then the secure fax machine started spitting out paper. "Must be the new sat images." Grant skimmed through them, tore off the lower section of one page, then went to the kitchen and handed it to James. "DJ, here are the frequencies for the CIA pilots' sat phones. Scott should be calling soon with call signs. And, DJ, take two radios."

"Will do, boss."

Grant joined Adler in the living room, then carried the new images to the dining room table and spread them out. "Oh shit," he grumbled.

"What'd you find?" Adler asked.

Grant flipped open the folder, took out the intel report, then sorted through the original images, placing one in particular next to the most recent. "Take a look at these. What do you see?"

"Other than the house, there's one vehicle."

"Right, Joe. According to the descriptions in the report, the agents had a four-wheel drive Nissan. Why isn't it showing in the latest images?" Picking up the latest intel report, Grant quickly read through it. "According to this, the SOG agents still haven't contacted the agents at the airport."

"Did they even *make* it to the property?"

"Good question."

"Looks like there's big trouble in River City," Adler quipped, taking the report from Grant.

"We'll review all the images and intel on the way to Gitmo. Listen, Joe, we've gotta haul soon, but I'm gonna call Grigori on the other secure phone. Standby for Scott's call."

"Will do."

Grant placed the call, and after two rings, he heard the familiar deep voice answer, "Hello."

"Hey, Grigori."

"My friend! We were just talking about you."

"Must be that ESP thing," Grant responded with a smile in his voice.

"Have you heard from Luke recently?"

"Talked with him two days ago. He's into his second month of pre-deployment training, which means he's got another sixteen months to go before operational deployment."

"Which will give you a worry-free sixteen months. Am I correct?"

"Yeah, I guess so. I'm gonna ask him to come this

way as soon as he can break free and take some leave. If that happens, we'll all get together. Sound good?"

"We would not miss it."

"Listen, Grigori, we're gonna be leaving soon. Specific details are being finalized. I'm waiting to hear from Scott."

"Have you told Luke?"

"Still deciding whether I should. He's got a lot on his plate."

"Can I give you my opinion, Grant?"

"Your opinions are *always* important."

"You should tell him. When the time comes for him to deploy, would you not want to know?"

Grant hesitated a moment. "Maybe, but I'll think about it. In the meantime, Scott has both of you on the notify list should anything happen."

"We will wait to hear from *you*, my good friend."

Grant turned when he heard the other phone ringing. Adler answered, then waved him over. Grant said, "Scott's on the other phone, Grigori. I've gotta go."

"Alexandra sends you a kiss."

"Give her a hug, Grigori."

"You be careful, Grant. You and your men be safe."

"Thanks, my friend." For now Grant had little time to think about talking with Luke. He took the phone from Adler. "What've you got for me, Scott?"

"I've confirmed your stop at Leeward Point in Gitmo and authorized refueling. Weather all the way to Gitmo and Colombia should be clear. I've also received the frequencies and call signs."

"I'll pass the weather info to Matt and Rob. Hold on

and I'll put DJ on. He already has the frequencies for the CIA pilots in Colombia." James took down the frequencies and call signs, then passed the phone to Grant, who glanced at his submariner. "We should be outta here in about twenty minutes, Scott. Once we land in Gitmo, I'll try to give you a quick call for any updates."

"I'll be here."

"In case I haven't told you lately, you're a good man, 'Charlie Brown.'"

Mullins chuckled. "I'll be waiting for your call, buddy. Be safe, all of you."

Grant gave the men a quick run through on Mullins' call, then, "DJ, fill us in on call signs."

"The *Roeti Island* is *Ironclad*, the choppers are Condor 1 and Condor 2 and we're Tango 8. I'll set frequencies once we're underway."

"Okay, that's it," Grant said. "I'll go put on my cammies." He headed to a back bedroom.

Adler watched him, knowing some kind of issue was bugging him. "Doc," Adler said pointing to the kitchen, "pour the coffee in a couple of thermos bottles, then finish putting water, sodas, sandwiches and snacks in the ice chest, enough to tide us over until reaching Gitmo. We'll grab some hot chow while we're there. But don't forget some Snickers."

"I'll be sure you have a few extra sandwiches, too, LT."

Adler gave a thumb's up then walked to the bedroom, and leaning against the doorframe asked Grant, "What's up? You thinking about calling Luke? Is that what Grigori suggested?"

Grant tucked his cammie shirt into his pants. "I suppose you're in agreement?"

"Your decision."

Carrying his jungle boots into the living room, Grant sat in the side chair just as one of the secure phones rang.

"What are the odds?" Adler questioned, handing it to Grant.

"Stevens."

"Sir, it's Luke."

Grant shot a surprised look at Adler. "How are ya, Luke?" Adler smiled, backed away, then joined the men in the kitchen.

"I'm good, sir. I . . . I just had a feeling I should give you a quick call."

"We must be on the same wavelength, Luke."

"So . . . so you *are* leaving?"

"We'll be outta here in about ten minutes. You understand that's all I can tell you, right?"

"Yes, sir."

"I don't think I mentioned it before, Luke, but you're on my 'to be notified' list, you and Grigori."

"Not mom?"

"Only you and Grigori." Grant glanced at his watch. "I'm gonna have to cut this short. Listen, once I'm back, I'll get word to you. Whenever you can take some leave, plan on coming here. Keep in mind that our next training class will begin the first week of April. I'll pay for your trip. Sound good?"

"Oh, yes, sir!"

"Quick question. How's the training?"

"Intense, but I'm enjoying the hell out of it!"

"I'm not surprised," Grant laughed. "Okay, gotta go. Take care of yourself, Luke."

"And you, sir. Please . . . take care. I'll be waiting for your call."

Grant laid down the phone, immediately laced up his boots, then sat quietly thinking about his son, as he took a moment to swipe fingers across his eyes.

Adler sat on the couch. "You okay?"

"Yeah, Joe," he said with a forced smile. "Listen, have the guys load the gear while I contact the security company."

The bulk of the gear was loaded into one of the SUVs, then Garrett and Draper drove it to the airfield. While they waited for the men, they filed a flight plan, then sitting in the *Herc's* cockpit, they started pre-flight.

Kalinin and James put the remaining gear in the second SUV, while Slade and Novak ensured nothing was left outside the three-car garage. Slade closed and locked the doors to the underground storage magazine. Then he and Novak unrolled a large rubber mat covering the floor of the first two garage spaces where the SUVs were usually parked, hiding the door embedded in the concrete.

Stalley and Milone jogged up the path, reporting the Quonset huts were secured. Garage doors were closed then the men went in the house, just as Grant was ending his call to the security firm. "Okay, guys. Let's get this show on the road." Boots pounded on the wood floor as A.T. raced out of the house.

The C-130 rumbled down the grass and dirt runway,

slowly rose, then circled Eagle 8 before continuing its climb to 25,000 feet, on a heading of 173°, for a three and a half hour flight to Gitmo.

Chapter 12

Aboard the *Herc*
Day 1 of Mission
Saturday
2015 Hours - Colombia Time

It was already two hours past sunset when Garrett adjusted the *Herc's* attitude, bringing it fifteen miles off Colombia's coastline. Draper notified Grant, "Proceeding along coast."

"Copy that." Grant glanced at his watch, then said to his men, "Confirm time is set back one hour." One by one, hands went up. "Okay. Sync at 2016 on one. Three, two, one."

As he looked up he noticed Kalinin leaning back against the jump seat with his eyes closed. Grant wondered, *Should I let him go through with it? His first mission jump?* For over three months the men of A.T. had trained him, taken him on multiple jumps, increasing the altitude a little at a time, teaching how to jump in a stack position. He'd shown no fear -- anxious, perhaps -- but no fear. Grant thought back to their first encounter. *How long ago was that? Who would've believed this was where fate would lead us?*

Adler elbowed him. "He'll be fine, Skipper." Grant smiled. He and his good friend somehow seemed to read each other's minds, and at just the right time.

He leaned back against the orange webbing of the jump seat and closed his eyes. Something besides worrying about Kalinin was bothering him even more, something about the mission. Maybe not the mission itself, but more the reason or reasons behind it. He mostly understood why the Mossad team and the CIA agents held a meeting. But if anything nefarious did happen to either team -- or both -- why did it? And how did Iran know about a supposed top secret meeting?

He snapped out of his thought process when he heard Adler's voice, "Listen up! Just a reminder: once our boots hit the ground, keep an eye out for slithery things. We might be okay close to the river, but there's a venomous pit viper known to be around the hills. They're nasty bastards, guys. They come in a variety of colors, and they've got large, needle-like fangs in the upper jaw."

"Oh, shit. Vampire snakes," Slade grumbled under his breath.

But A.T. was already prepared for the jungle environment and terrain. Strands of paracord had been tied around the bottom of their pant legs, securing them to their jungle boots. Shirts were tucked in, cuffs buttoned. Black and green camouflage paint streaked their faces.

Out of the corner of his eye Grant spotted Draper coming from the flight deck. He stopped in front of Grant, and covering his mic, said, "Received confirmation the LHD's in position. Choppers are standing by." Grant gave an okay sign, then passed the word to his men. He glanced at James, who gave him a thumb's up, confirming sat phone frequencies had been set.

Draper continued walking through the cargo bay prepared to open the cargo bay doors, when he heard Garrett's voice in his headset, and replied, "Roger." Pausing in the aisle, he held up two fingers and announced loudly, "Depressurizing in two!"

The men stood in the aisle, snapped their aviator-style masks to their helmets, adjusted the O2 flowing from belt tanks, then adjusted goggles. They quickly went through final checks again, repeating the entire process, ensuring the integrity of fasteners on the ram-air chutes, checking the reserve chutes, giving the crotch straps one more tug. NVGs were raised and locked in place. Weapons were secured.

Standing by the control panel, Draper advised Garrett he was prepared to open the cargo bay doors. Except for green lights illuminating the flight deck, and small red lights along the cargo bay, all interior lights were extinguished.

The sound of the four turboprop engines changed, as Garrett started deceleration, bringing the speed down to one hundred thirty knots. Draper pressed the switch. A loud, high-pitched motor whined. The cargo door raised, and the ramp started lowering. Noise dramatically increased. A tremendous rush of cold air, along with a smell of jet fuel swept through the cargo bay.

Once the door was fully raised and the lowered ramp was horizontal and level with the cargo bay deck, Draper tugged on his safety harness before cautiously walking onto the ramp. He made visual inspections of both sides and the locking mechanisms. Satisfied the ramp was secured, he moved back toward the control panel, alerted Garrett, then his eyes went to each of his teammates. Holding a hand overhead, he gave a thumb's up. Each man signaled the same, knowing it was time to keep their focus on him. He glanced at his watch then held up two fingers. Two minutes to jump.

The Team attached their rucksacks to their reserve chutes. Grouped in close proximity to one another, they each mentally pictured the jump, and trying to stay loose, they rolled their shoulders, stretched their arms overhead. Twenty-four thousand feet below was nothing but the blackness of the Pacific Ocean. They'd be under canopy for close to forty miles.

The *Herc* began a slow, wide turn. Draper got the Team's attention then held up a fist, indicating thirty seconds until jump.

As Grant edged his way onto the ramp, he paused, laid a hand on Kalinin's shoulder, then gave him a nod. Kalinin responded in kind. The rest of the Team moved closer. The *Herc* shuddered as it flew through brief patches of turbulence. The men spread their legs, helping to maintain their balance.

Getting final confirmation from Garrett, Draper folded his arm across his chest, and in one swift motion, swung his arm out to the side, pointing to the exit.

With adrenaline surging, Team A.T. dove head first within seconds of one another, falling into the dark emptiness. A tremendous blast of cold air pressed against their bodies. The sound of wind whistled by.

Seconds after jumping, D-rings were pulled, releasing the black ram-air chutes. A brief rustling of material sounded just before the chutes fully opened, the sudden force violently jerking bodies. Crotch straps dug in. As they began swaying gently in their harnesses, they immediately lowered NVGs.

Team A.T. started maneuvering in the light wind, using the toggles to adjust their direction, finally coming together to form up in a stack, with Grant in the lowest position. It was up to him, using the GPS and compass, to set their course, to guide them close to the LZ alongside the river.

On-board the *Herc,* Draper knelt on the ramp, watching through NVGs, counting each chute as it opened. He confirmed with Garrett that it was a good jump. Walking backwards to the control panel, he kept staring out into the darkness, picturing his friends being carried by the wind to their objective. Finally, he pressed the switch. The ramp slowly started raising, the door lowering. Once both were secured he hurried to the flight deck, resuming his place in the right seat.

Garrett pushed the thrusters forward, slowly increasing power, bringing the aircraft close to max speed. The *Herc* instantly responded, beginning its return to Gitmo.

Chapter 13

The port city of Buenaventura was behind them, its lights fading below the western horizon. They were passing over the next landmark, the first bend in the Rio Danubio. *Next crossing's another one and a half miles,* Grant thought.

As the second bend in the river passed beneath them, a distant low glow on the southeast horizon gave him another landmark, the small village of San Cipriano. He glanced at the compass, and continued heading east.

C'mon! C'mon! Where the hell is it?! he thought anxiously, noticing the coordinates on the GPS. *There it is.* He pulled down on the toggle, steering more to the left, breaking away from the team. They took his lead and one by one broke away, leaving plenty of room between one another.

A quick glance at the altimeter on the top of his reserve chute showed he was at one hundred feet. At fifty feet he pulled down on both toggles, causing the chute to begin stalling. With his knees together and slightly bent, he pulled down a little more, then finally, at ten feet, he pulled down hard on both toggles. The chute stalled, and he touched down, taking a few, short, running steps before immediately turning to gather his chute.

The men touched down within seconds of one another, then working quickly, unhooked their rucksacks from their reserve chutes. Foregoing the normal figure-eighting of shroud lines, they gathered their chutes, and hurried toward Grant who was nearing the tree line.

He raised his NVGs, took a knee, and whispering, asked, "Everyone okay?" Thumbs went up. He looked directly at Kalinin. "Nick?"

Just above a whisper Kalinin responded, "That was great!" Grant just smiled before getting down to business. "Get jump gear packed and ready weapons," he whispered, glancing at his submariner. "We're moving out in fifteen."

Removing his gloves, he took his night vision glasses from the rucksack, steadied himself on a knee, then began scanning the narrowest crossing point of the thirty-foot wide, slow-moving river. They'd use the thick brush and tree cover right up to the sloping bank, staying under tree branches that extended out over the river by at least ten feet. The water depth was shallow, maybe just above their boots.

Those river rocks might be slicker than snot, Grant thought.

Adler scoped out the opposite bank, and whispered, "Entire opposite bank's covered in pebbles and rocks, but the forest is, maybe, twenty feet beyond it."

Grant lowered the glasses, then looked at his men, all in tune with one another, all in tune with the mission. Milone, Kalinin, and James had taken up defensive positions, holding their weapons, keeping eyes on through their NVGs. Slade was wiping down the razor sharp machete, aware that he had to keep sound to a minimum when he cut through the jungle brush—and possibly slithery things. Stalley had closed his medical bag, and was cleaning the camera lens, readying it for the first picture. Novak was adjusting his sniper rifle's AN/PVS high-power scope, specifically for night ops, a Starlight, with a six hundred fifty yard detection range.

With a snap of his fingers, Grant got the men's attention then motioned them farther into the trees. With them gathered around him, he unfolded a sat image, laid it on the ground, took a pen light from his vest, then switched on the pen's red light, aiming it on the location of a waterfall just north of them. He located their present position. "We're here. Target's coordinates are here, just about due east." He slid a finger across the image, then tapped an area. "We can come in from behind the house then do recons. That'll be head-on with the road leading in from the highway."

"You want me to do the first recon?" Slade asked.

"We'll play it by ear. I'll be at your six with the GPS." Grant pointed to two separate places on the image. "It looks like two clearings where I can check the coordinates." He sealed the image in a plastic bag, then put it in his vest.

They had three quarters of a mile to cover, three quarters of a mile of jungle. Grant signaled his men forward. Slade took the lead, with Milone and Stalley covering their sixes. Cautiously, the men stepped into the shallow, slow-moving water.

Chapter 14

We've gotta be getting close, Grant thought, as he looked overhead, finally seeing a clearing in the canopy. He held up a fist, bringing everyone to a stop, then tapped Slade's shoulder. They'd been walking on level ground, making it nearly impossible to see any sign of a clearing around the property.

He checked the GPS. *Sixty yards.* With his men watching him, he indicated the distance with his fingers. His intention was to approach from the rear of the house. Slade checked the compass, then held it for Grant to see. Grant nodded, then waved everyone forward.

Finally, Slade brought everyone to a stop. The Team automatically took a knee, then Slade pointed straight ahead toward a complete view of the back of the house. Only partial views were of each side.

Grant and Adler crept cautiously around trees and brush, then got on their bellies, and raised their NVGs. From their positions, and using their glasses, they scanned as much of the property as was allowed, mainly looking for any signs of life. Nothing. No one. Focusing on the rear of the house, Grant noticed there wasn't a door, but there were two broken windows. From Simmons' description, broken windows may not mean anything. But Grant's instincts warned him to be prepared. Shit could happen in a heartbeat.

He signaled Slade to scope out the north side, looking specifically for the Israelis' vehicle. Crouching low, Slade moved cautiously until he had a clear view. Within minutes he reported to Grant that the green vehicle was still parked in the same location on the north side as was seen in the sat image, but there wasn't any sign of the agents' vehicle.

They had to stick to the original plan and begin a recon. There was too much open ground to cover across the front and south side. He tapped Adler's shoulder, then signaling with a thumb pointing back, they returned to the Team. It was time to move.

*

Staying just within the cover of the jungle, they made their way closer to the house. The men took positions on either side of Grant. Except for he and Adler who were looking through the glasses, the rest of the Team took defensive postures.

Novak lifted the rifle strap over his head as he was getting comfortable on his butt. With his knees drawn in, he aimed the rifle, then adjusted the night scope.

While Grant was surveilling the property, he realized they had to change tactics for the recon. Novak had to be repositioned to give himself a clear view of the entire front of the house and road. The likelihood of anyone approaching from other than the road seemed remote, but they couldn't take the chance.

He motioned the men closer, then whispered into his throat mic. "Mike, set up inside the north tree line just beyond where the van's parked. We'll wait for your all clear. Ken, Vince, look for any signs of tire marks or any disruption to trees and brush along that same side. Don't penetrate too deeply into the jungle. DJ, Doc, take the south side," he pointed. "Nick, Joe, and I will take the north side; once everyone's in position, we'll check the van, then the house. Questions?" Silence. "Mike—go."

Novak took off, staying within the trees, as he hurried to find the best position.

After several minutes they finally heard him in their earpieces, "About fifteen yards beyond van. All clear. But there's a shitload of spent casings everywhere. Rounds struck van multiple times. Copy?"

"Copy," Grant responded, then with a sick feeling, he thought, *Firefight.* He pointed to Slade and Milone.

As the two took off, Slade pressed the PTT, "Mike, on our way toward you. Copy?"

"Copy."

Grant waited, then hearing Slade confirm that he was beginning the recon while Milone guarded his six, Grant responded, "Copy." He signaled James and Stalley. James would position himself at the front south corner, Stalley the rear. Once they confirmed, Grant pressed the PTT. "Ken, you see anything? Over."

"Thirty yards in. Found evidence someone may have used a machete. Wait one." He took out his NV glasses and looked farther into the jungle. "Eyes on the same type cuts maybe twenty yards ahead. Want me to continue on?"

"Negative, but can you tell how long ago?"

Slade examined a few of the cut twigs and palm fronds. "I'd say at least a day."

"Okay. Come back and assume your position." *What the hell happened? Who could've cut their way through, and why?* Thinking about the spent casings, he worried,

Ambush?! He pressed the PTT, notifying everyone, "On our way to vehicle." He, Adler, and Kalinin cautiously walked closer to the van. Adler pointed down, drawing their attention to empty shell casings.

While Grant and Adler continued toward the van's rear, Kalinin looked into the cargo area through the windshield. What he saw turned his stomach. Hurrying toward Grant and Adler, he pressed the PTT to notify everyone, then gruffly whispered, "Bodies inside van."

Grant looked toward the trail cut through the jungle, and silently confirmed, *Ambush!*

Adler flipped up his NVGs, and brushed past Grant, stepping near the van's rear door. He noticed dark stains along the bumper where blood had either dripped from under the door or from bodies being dragged into the van. As former EOD, Adler wasn't taking any chances. Holding his pen light, he shined the red light around the door, looking for possible wires. Finding none, he cautiously opened the door. The smell nearly knocked him back. "Jesus."

Grant held his breath, then stood closer to the opening, seeing blood-stained floorboards and clothes. From the angle the three bodies were lying, he could only recognize one. "Rabin. The Israelis." His mind whirled before he said, "One's missing. The woman. The woman's not here." He looked toward the house as he pressed the PTT. "Three Israelis dead. We're heading to house." Though shocked by the news, the Team didn't question, and remained quiet.

With NVGs in place, and with Adler in the lead, they hustled toward the front of the house, stopping just to the side of the door.

Adler started reaching for the doorknob, when something caught his eye. He motioned for Grant and Kalinin to look at the ground, at scattered, empty shell casings, and a wide, dried blood trail, smeared with dirt, leading under the door. There wasn't time to speculate, but by the amount of blood, whoever was inside was probably dead. With caution prevailing, Adler quickly inspected around the doorframe, looked for signs of wires, then signaled Grant with a thumb's up.

Prepared for CQB (Close Quarters Battle), Kalinin tapped Grant's shoulder, signaling he was ready.

With Adler's eyes on him, Grant nodded.

Novak briefly focused his scope on the three men, and seeing they were in position, he whispered into his mic, "They're going in."

Chapter 15

Adler turned the doorknob just enough to feel the latch release, then holding his weapon across the front of his body, he took a step back. With a quick, powerful kick, the door flew open. He rushed in, went right, with Grant and Kalinin going left and center, aiming their weapons, scanning the entire room.

Grant glanced down at the floor, with his eyes following a dried, dark stain, a bloody trail that led to a body sprawled out near the wall. He motioned Kalinin toward him, then pointed two fingers at his own NVGs, then to Kalinin, then the bedroom. Kalinin gave a quick nod, then immediately left.

Adler rushed from the opposite side of the room. "Clear!"

Kalinin called from the bedroom, "Bedroom clear."

Grant knelt next to the body, running photos of the agents through his brain. "Fuck! It's Kaufman."

"Damn," Adler said, shaking his head.

Grant pressed the PTT. "One agent dead. No other bodies. Have any weapons been found?"

Responses came back: "Negative."

"DJ, need you now. Everyone else hold positions."

James hurried in. "Yeah, boss?"

"DJ, the new encryption for the sat phone is set, right?"

"Affirm, boss." (Every twenty-four hours all DoD sat phones were switched to the same new encrypted number.)

"Go ahead and contact the CIA pilots. I'll talk with them." While James readied the sat phone, Grant backed away, motioning Kalinin and Adler closer.

"Now what the hell do we do?" Adler asked, resting his MP5 against his shoulder.

"Depends on CIA. But the bodies have gotta be taken outta here. A chopper can be here in less than a half hour."

James walked closer, handing the phone to Grant, advising, "It's Agent Nyland."

"Agent Nyland, Grant Stevens, sir."

"What've you found, Captain?"

"Sir, I'm sorry to tell you, but Agent Kaufman's dead. He was shot. We found his body in the house."

"Holy Christ! And the others?!"

"We only surveilled and walked a limited area of the property, but there wasn't any sign of them."

"Hostages," Nyland mumbled, with obvious distress in his voice.

"That's what we suspect."

"And what about the Israelis?"

"The bodies of three males were in their van, all shot. I was only able to identify Rabin. There wasn't any sign of Neman, the woman. Both teams must've put up a helluva firefight, sir. We found a helluva lot of spent casings, but what we haven't found are weapons, so we suspect they were confiscated by the attackers."

"Dammit, *dammit*," Nyland grumbled. "Captain, did you find any trace of any other vehicle having been on the property?"

"There are tire tracks in front of the house, but they could've been made by the van the first time the Mossad team scoped out the property. There's no way to tell. But my men found a trail cut through the jungle. If that was made by the attackers, they could've left a vehicle on another road or trail."

"Hold on a minute, Captain, while I speak with Agent Sands. Chuck, hand me the last image of the property." While Sands retrieved the image, Nyland gave him a shortened version of the attack. Sands handed him the image then sunk down on a seat opposite him.

Nyland laid the paper on the table between him and Sands, then asked Grant, "What side of the property was that trail?"

"North, the side with the van."

Nyland pointed to the area for Sands. "Chuck, call Langley. Fill them in. Then, see if they've got any U-2 or sat images showing a vehicle or vehicles in this vicinity." Sands went to the cockpit for the extra sat phone.

"Okay, Captain. Anything else?"

"Yes, sir. I don't know if you're aware, but there's an LHD positioned off the coast with choppers waiting. I'd like to suggest that one be sent here to pick up the bodies. It's the humane thing to do, sir."

"I agree, but State will most likely talk it over with the Israelis, you know, get their permission, opinions. Will you and your men accompany the bodies to the ship?"

"It'd be an honor," Grant said, then hesitated before adding, "but I don't believe our mission here is over yet."

"And you have approval to continue?"

"Not exactly, sir. Our main mission was to find the agents, which we obviously haven't accomplished. But if I understood Director Simmons correctly, continuing be-

yond that was, well, left open. In any case, let me give
you our exact coordinates to pass on to the chopper crew
in case that's approved. They're aware of our call sign."

Nyland took down the numbers, then said, "Stay
where you are. I'll call as soon as I hear from Langley."

"We'll be here."

Chapter 16

Grant hooked the phone on his belt. "Joe, Nick, outside." He pressed the PTT, gave his men a quick run-through, then said, "Doc, need you. DJ, take Doc's position."

Stalley came around the corner. "Boss?"

"Doc, take pictures, inside and out, and start at the van. Have Ken show you the trail, then tell him, Vince and Mike to hold positions for now." Stalley left.

"What are you thinking?" Adler asked.

"Gimme a minute, Joe." Raising his NVGs, then hooking a thumb under the rifle strap on his shoulder, Grant walked a few paces away from the house, while thinking of his conversation with Nyland, who he told the mission wasn't over. He couldn't believe CIA would order them out of Colombia, not with three agents and a Mossad woman missing, and with four deaths. *Were others injured? Would the body count rise?*

He glanced at his submariner, figuring the time since the attack. He guessed it was the Israelis who were hit first. He looked north, toward the trail. Whoever set up the ambush designed it so there was no possibility of crossfire, somebody who was experienced in firefights, particularly in ambushes. What were the odds that a guerrilla group had perpetrated the attack? He shook his head. *It had to be the Quds Force.*

Nyland gave no mention of intercepts by CIA or the Israelis. *Why not? Why the silence?* Considering the seriousness of the attack, somebody in Colombia had to report it to Iran.

He stopped pacing as a sudden thought crossed his

mind. *What if that Iranian sleeper agent had already slipped into the country in one of the Ural trucks? Is he the reason the Quds knew about the meeting? What if he's got total control of whatever's planned, and communication with Iran is unnecessary?* "So where does that leave *you*, Stevens," he said under his breath. But his mind went back to the woman. *Neman. Ashira Neman. She's Mossad. Would her training help keep her alive? Or would that make her even more vulnerable if the Quds knew or found out?* A sudden chill went through him.

The sat phone alerted him to an incoming call. "Stevens."

"Captain, Gary Nyland. First, approval's been given for Condor 1 to assist. Lieutenants Zimmer and Daikin will be the pilots. I would think they should be departing any time now."

"Thank you, sir." Grant looked at his watch then turned toward the house. Getting his men's attention, he twirled two fingers high overhead, then gave a thumb's up.

"Now," Nyland continued, "Langley reviewed earlier images from the U-2, but no vehicles were spotted along that east side."

"Damn."

"Understand, Captain, that the U-2 wasn't sent up until we reported that the agents hadn't contacted us."

"By then the UFs would've hauled ass."

"UFs?"

"Unfriendlies. Sir, wait one, please." He took a knee, laid the phone on the ground, then removed a sat image stored in the plastic bag. He zeroed in on the area north. "The freakin' mine." He grabbed the phone. "Sir, Director Simmons informed me there's a gold mine about two miles from here, a mine being controlled by the Quds Force, a mine where he suspects a cache of weapons may be stockpiled."

"You think . . .?"

"There's one way to be certain, and that's for us to proceed with our mission."

"That's what I was about to tell you. You've been given authorization to continue."

"That's great to hear. Thanks. Am I to contact you once the chopper has departed from here?"

"We'd appreciate it."

"Very well, sir. Thanks again." Grant disconnected the call, pressed the PTT, updated his men, then added, "DJ, chopper should be underway. Doc, Vince, be ready to assist crew with the bodies. Everyone else remain on alert." A sound of a chopper could draw attention—unwanted, dangerous attention.

Maintaining their positions, the Team waited for Condor 1.

Chapter 17

Sunday
Day 2 of Mission
0020 Hours

On the flight deck of the LHD, Condor 1 was prepared for takeoff. Its twin turboshaft engines were set to
idle, ensuring the rpms stayed around ninety-six percent.

Inside the cargo bay, the gunner positioned the link
belt for his .50 cal machine gun, and checked that the
"brass catchers" were secured to the weapon, ensuring
the canvas bags would catch all spent cartridges. Swivel-
ing the gun side to side, he checked that the primary observation sectors were the normal sixty degrees off the
chopper's nose, going all the way to the rear.

The crew chief disconnected the communication ca-
bles, removed the wheel chocks, then climbed aboard,
confirming with the cockpit crew they were ready for
takeoff.

A motor whined, raising the steel ramp. The crew
chief took his position just behind the cockpit near a 3x3
open window, opposite the gunner. He adjusted his
leather holster holding his .45, then swiveled the M16
around to his back. With NVGs in place, he leaned an
arm on the window frame.

After checking the surrounding area, Lieutenant Chet
Zimmer and Lieutenant Les Daikin both confirmed it
was clear. Zimmer engaged the blades. Engines roared
as he slowly lifted the collective. Condor 1 rose above

the deck. Zimmer made a pedal adjustment, moved the cyclic left, and set the chopper's course to due east.

*

Flying NOE (Nap of the Earth), Zimmer made instant adjustments, and while skillfully maintaining the same speed, he used the collective for modifying power, and the cyclic for precise pitch attitude changes. Below the Seahawk, trees, brush, all plant life swirled violently as it sped by.

Closing in on the coordinates, Zimmer adjusted the collective, and began decreasing speed. In the left seat, copilot Daikin contacted James, advising Condor 1 was three miles from coordinates. With the IR (Infrared) searchlight on, and only visible through NVGs, Daikin manually adjusted the control.

Hearing the chopper, Grant ran to the opposite side of the property. Looking through his NVGs, he caught sight of the IR searchlight, and turned on his pen light's red light. Holding it high overhead, he moved it slowly side to side as the chopper approached.

Condor 1's nose rose slightly, as Zimmer brought it to a hover position, while ensuring his forward airspeed was sufficient, and being careful not to apply too much throttle. Rotor blades kicked up massive amounts of debris, nearly obliterating the LZ. Zimmer utilized the IGE (In Ground Effect), the cushion of air beneath the blades to give additional lift to the Seahawk as it descended. Finally, its wheels settled onto the ground. He set the twin turboshaft engines to idle. He and Daikin raised their

NVGs, seeing Grant heading toward them.

As Grant ran to the open doorway, two crew members jumped out, each holding body bags. Grant shouted, "One body's in the house, three in the van!" He pointed to Stalley and Milone. "My men will assist you!" The crewmen took off. Grant raised his NVGs, climbed aboard, then leaned into the cockpit, offering a hand to Zimmer then Daikin. "Gentlemen, nice to meet you. We appreciate your assistance."

"Our pleasure, sir," Zimmer said, "especially considering the unfortunate circumstances."

Grant pursed his lips, nodded, then asked, "What was your flight time?"

"Just about twenty minutes, sir," Zimmer replied.

"You must've had the pedal to the metal."

"That we did, sir."

Grant turned serious again. "I understand that you and Condor 2 will be on stand-by for when it's time to extract us."

"That's correct, sir," Daikin said. "Lieutenants Weinrich and Basquez will be flying Condor 2."

"Very well." Hearing footsteps, Grant turned toward the door, seeing the first two body bags being carried by the two crewmen, Stalley, and Milone. Grant offered his hand again to the pilots. "I'd better give them some room. Thanks again. Have a safe flight, gentlemen."

"Thank you, sir, and good luck."

Grant gave a quick two finger salute, then jumped from the chopper.

In less than five minutes, the last two body bags and crew were aboard the chopper. Zimmer engaged the blades, opened the throttle completely, then slowly lifted the collective. The turboshaft engines roared as he continued lifting the collective, applying more power. Condor 1 got lighter on its wheels. Making a pedal adjustment, and simultaneously adjusting the cyclic and collective, Zimmer brought Condor 1 higher above the jungle floor. As its nose dipped, beginning forward flight, Grant gave a final, full salute.

Chapter 18

"Skipper," Adler said, mustering alongside Grant, "when Vince and Doc were removing the bodies, they found four bullet-resistant vests piled behind the front seats."

"Are you kidding me?!"

"I know. You'd think they would've taken that extra step."

"Something else that's gotta go in the report," Grant quietly said.

"What now?" Adler asked.

"Now? We need to get the hell outta here, Joe. But first I've gotta call Agent Nyland. Listen, keep the guys on watch. The chopper could've attracted someone's attention."

"You planning on driving to the next target?" Adler asked, pointing toward the van.

"Negative. It's about two miles to that mine. We'll follow the trail, take the same route those bastards took, then set up surveillance during mine work hours, which should be close to sunrise." He unhooked the phone from his belt, then elbowed Adler. "As a just in case, Joe, check the van. See if it's good to go. Oh, and pick up a variety of those spent casings." Grant placed the call.

"Nyland."

"Grant Stevens, sir. I'm confirming the chopper departed about six minutes ago with four bodies on-board."

"All right, Captain," Nyland sighed.

"This is just an FYI, but the flight time of the LHD took twenty minutes. It should take about the same going back. Sir, if there's nothing else, I'd better close. We're getting ready to head to the next target."

"Understood, but I've got a couple of items. Neither D.C. nor the Israelis have received any demands from the attackers. What that means is anyone's guess."

"I had hoped we could've gotten some answers. But what about intercepts?"

"Not a damn thing pertaining to this operation."

"That's pretty worrisome. The Iranians must've planned this down to a T."

"Let's hope they screw up, Captain; otherwise, I don't know how it'll play out, especially on your end." Silence. Nyland finally asked, "If there are updates, should we contact you on the sat phone?"

"Uh, that *might* not be a good idea, sir."

"Of course; don't know what I was thinking. I was also asked to pass on to you that the cargo ship remains on schedule and is due to arrive in port Monday. No definite time was given."

"Monday. We'll see where that leads," Grant mumbled.

"Care to explain, Captain?"

"Uh, no, sir. But you didn't hear what you think you just heard. Okay?"

Nyland chuckled, "Didn't hear a thing. Listen, we've received orders to depart after this call. I'm afraid you're all on your own, Captain."

"Been there before, sir."

"Look, give us a call once you're back home. Drinks are on us. Okay?"

"Sounds good. Look forward to it."

"Godspeed."

As Grant walked toward Adler and Kalinin who were by the front door, Adler said, "We're ready to haul, Skipper." Grant nodded, but giving no response, Adler asked, "What's whirling around in that brain?"

"Agent Nyland reported that no one's received any demands from the Quds."

"And? We're guesstimating it's only been around fifteen hours."

"I know. I know. But what if we don't find the hostages at the mine? What if there was another plan, like transporting them to the cargo ship, which is due in port on Monday?"

"Wait! What?! This is a helluva time to have second thoughts."

"Jesus, Grant," Kalinin piped up, "we can't be in two places at the same time."

"Neither of you have to tell me what I already know," Grant snapped, but then he immediately regretted his retort. "Apologies, guys. Listen, we'll stick with the original plan, then see where it leads. Joe, tell me about the van."

"I started it up while the chopper was here. Gas tank's almost full. I've got the key. The cargo bed's kinda what you'd expect, considering. And before you ask, Doc took a shitload of pictures." Adler patted a pocket of his utility vest. "We've all picked up some of the casings."

Grant looked toward each of his men, most of whom were still standing watch. "Then I guess we're ready." While he, Adler and Kalinin started walking toward the trail, he pressed the PTT. "Let's go."

Chapter 19

Pereira, Colombia
Sunday
0025 Hours - Local Time

Located on the northwest coast, Santa Marta's supply
station injected the oil into a transportation pipeline.
That began the oil's journey through multiple cities and
pump stations, en route to its final destination of Buenaventura. Along the route it would pass through block
valve stations built every twenty to thirty miles along the
route. The stations were the first line of protection for
that pipeline and the valuable liquid flowing inside it.
Operators at each location had the capability to isolate
any segment of the line for maintenance work, and more
importantly, to isolate a rupture or leak.

Six hundred miles south of Santa Marta, the pipeline
passed outside the city of Pereira, where one of the many
block valve stations was located. Thousands of acres of
open land surrounded most of the locations. Pereira was
one of those, with the land specifically designated as
grazing pastures for cattle, since Colombia was one of
the largest exporters of beef in the world. Smaller pastures were grazing land for goats, used for milk and food
sources for the locals.

An eight-foot high, chain link fence surrounded the
station. Bright security lights and recording devices were
spaced at each corner, five feet above the fencing. Small
pebbles were spread across the ground inside the fencing,
with a layer spread right up to the block valve itself.

Built thirty feet away and opposite the security gate, the operations center was a single-level cinder block structure, with four windows across the front. A regular steel door was its only access. A loudspeaker was fastened to the top corner of the building.

Carlos Rojas was one of four men who had operated the Pereira block valve station for the past five years. During that time they had ordered maintenance on ten different segments of the line and reported nine incidents of leaks, the last one twenty-three days earlier.

An hour before he assumed watch, he reviewed the logs from the previous shift. Then, using his access key, he entered the fenced-in area, made a close up inspection of the block valve, then returned to the building, just as the wind picked up.

Before settling in, he unscrewed the cap from a thermos, poured a cold, dark-colored brew into a coffee cup, then resealed the cap. He looked toward the camera monitors around the console while drinking two consecutive mouthfuls of the aguapanela. Licking his lips, he savored the mixture of sweet sugar cane and lemon, wiped the back of a hand across his mouth, then went to the console.

Rolling out a chair, he glanced at a clock above the door. *Five more hours,* he sighed. Sitting in front of the wide, Formica-top, curved console, he kept a watchful eye on security camera monitors, along with a multitude of switches, buttons, and gauges.

At 0115 the recording devices registered noises along the east side fence. Rojas focused on one of the monitors, then turning a dial slowly, he adjusted the camera, pointing it along the fence. With the wind picking up, anything could have set off the sensitive devices. It was not unusual for a wild animal, or even a goat, to stray onto the property, but the bright lights usually prevented any such intrusion—usually.

The shrill sound of an alarm startled him. Something or someone had either made contact with or had actually breached the fence. His eyes immediately focused on a section of the console and a blinking red light, indicating the south side fence. Quickly adjusting the camera, he spotted a white goat, lying next to the fence. He shut off the alarm, then adjusting the camera again, zoomed in on the animal, seeing its tongue hanging out a side of its mouth. He had no doubt it was dead. The question now was whether he should leave it for the next shift, or deal with it now and prevent wild animals from causing additional problems. Opting to drag it away from the compound, he drew his Beretta, ensured the safety was off, shoved it into his side holster, then left the building.

He had walked halfway to the fence, when five men, dressed in jungle cammies, rushed from behind the building. Rojas swung around, reached for his pistol, but was immediately cut down by a barrage of AK-47 rounds. He was dead before he hit the ground.

Two of the attackers rushed into the building, and began shutting down the security system. Soon after, three others broke the gate's lock, then dragged in canvas sacks.

Within thirty minutes, all tasks were completed. Sticks of dynamite had been placed strategically around the block valve assembly, and in full view. The explosives were being used as a ruse to draw attention, but that was only partially true. The attackers were prepared to use RPGs, ensuring destruction of the station and operations building, or anyone in the vicinity.

Up and down the pipeline the same well orchestrated attacks were planned at specific locations. Attackers were all members of local guerrilla organizations. But remaining in the background at each location were three to four men of the Quds Force, who had trained the guerrillas and directed the operation. For the time being, the Quds had to wait for demands to be sent to the Colombian and U.S. governments.

The first day after such demand was sent, nothing would be destroyed, but to prove the Quds had control, they would shutdown a major pump station. Then, each ensuing day when a demand was not met, either a pump station or block valve station would be attacked. While that meant oil flow would immediately be interrupted, the Colombians would soon realize that with each ensuing day and attack, the costs for repairs would soar. Maintenance workers' lives would be put in jeopardy. How many would even be willing to attempt those repairs?

Beyond that, the disruption of oil exports would have a devastating affect on the economy.

For Shahbaz, the plan, while still in its early stages, had gone better than expected. The mission was destined to succeed. Iran would not only have control of Venezuela's oil, but soon Colombia's.

Chapter 20

Israel Government Offices
Jerusalem
Sunday
0930 Hours - Local Time - 8 hours ahead of Colombia

With his arms behind his back, Prime Minister Josef Peritz walked slowly around the long oval conference table, waiting for his ministers to arrive for their usual Sunday weekly meeting. He couldn't shake the feelings of both anger and grief since hearing the news. Over and over he ran through his mind the number killed, the number missing -- Mossad and CIA agents. *How in the hell did it happen? It was only to be a meeting, an exchange of intelligence. What the Americans decided to do after that had been left up to them.*

He looked up, hearing hurried footsteps along the corridor. "Prime Minister," Mossad Director Samuel Chaikin said as he entered the room.

"You have further news?" Peritz asked as Chaikin walked toward him.

"Not as much as we were hoping for, but Secretary McKinley reported the helicopter was transporting the bodies to the ship. I would think it has landed by now."

Peritz was quiet a moment. "Samuel, I would like to have those bodies returned soon."

"It is my opinion, Mr. Prime Minister, that we hold off on that."

"Go on."

"While we are certain it was the Quds Force who

perpetrated that attack, and not a guerrilla group, we must play it safe for the time being. Secretary McKinley informed me that it was a team of special operations men who found the carnage, and had requested the helicopter. Those men have been authorized to track the attackers, and find the hostages."

"Samuel, we are talking about the Quds Force. Does anyone believe the hostages are still alive?"

"Mr. Prime Minister, we must give the special ops men some time."

With frustration in his voice, Peritz asked, "And in the meantime, Samuel, what is going to happen in Colombia? What are the Iranians planning?"

"Secretary McKinley and I discussed all likely possibilities. Each one can cause major problems, and not only in Colombia. But it is believed they have plans to attack or at least take control of a pipeline. I understand CIA will be examining satellite images to confirm that either way."

Peritz cast his eyes downward. "Will we be taking any action against Iran? Have you thought about that?"

"I have. I will meet with members of the Kidon ("tip of the spear"). We know that Behnam Khorasani is in charge of the operation."

"So, has he become your number one target?"

"For now, yes."

"Have you discussed this with the Americans? I mean about him being a target."

"Not yet. There will most likely be more, and I would like to have additional names before doing so. We have worked with secretaries of defense in the past before we ran an assassination operation. This time would be no different, especially since they have men working their own mission inside Colombia."

"Exactly what is their mission?"

"Rescue hostages."

"And beyond that?"

"It was not discussed, but just as Mossad's missions, one mission can lead to many continuations, Mr. Prime Minister."

"I see. All right, Samuel." He laid a hand on Chaikin's shoulder. "I want you to remain for part of the meeting, so you can detail the events and answer questions."

"Yes, sir."

Peritz continued walking toward one of several windows, then pointed to a clear, blue sky. "All one has to do, Samuel, is look at that. For a fraction of a moment, it can make all the evil in the world seem to disappear—but only for a fraction of a moment."

Chapter 21

Valle del Cauca, Colombia
Sunday
0110 Hours

Following the trail cut by the attackers, the trek from
the property had taken less time than expected. Slade
held up a fist. Each man dropped to a knee. He motioned Grant closer, pointed, then leaning toward him,
whispered, "Clearing, twenty yards."

Grant turned to his men, then held up a hand, motioning for them to wait. Stalley and Milone covered their
sixes. Adler removed his night scope, keeping eyes on
Grant and Slade, as the two eased their way forward.
Approaching the end of the trail, they finally noticed
what was little more than another beaten-down path running perpendicular to them, just wide enough for a medi-
um-size vehicle. But what got their attention was a dirt
road directly across from them, heading north.

They both took a knee, then looked up and down the
path. Confident it was clear, and with weapons ready,
they moved onto the edge of the path. Standing back to
back they scanned the area. The only movement was a
flutter of leaves and palm fronds.

Grant whispered to Slade, "Look for tires tracks."

They walked in opposite directions, and had only
gone about thirty feet, when Grant thought, *There's nothing here.* He headed back, and snapped his fingers, getting Slade's attention. As Slade headed toward him,
Grant pointed to him, then the dirt road. Slade nodded,

then started up the road, with Grant providing cover.

Within five minutes, Slade came back, and standing near Grant, whispered, "There's a shitload of tire tracks. Must've been what the U-2 picked up. But there was one set about twenty yards in from here that veered deeper into the trees and brush. No indication the vehicle continued forward, so I'd say it was backed out."

The two returned to the Team, where Grant removed the sat image and pen light from his vest, then checked the distance and coordinates. He pointed to the dirt road. "That's to the mine. It shouldn't take us long."

*

A sound of rushing water signaled A.T. was nearing the mine. Grant tapped Slade's shoulder, then turned and stopped his men, before taking out his glasses. About forty yards away was the edge of the tree line, and beyond that the river. Its width had narrowed to no more than three feet, as it cascaded over and around a barricade of rocks, then flowed into a pool, before slowly continuing south.

Grant removed the vial from his vest, held it so the men knew what he was planning, then put it back in his vest. The men immediately moved off the dirt road, taking defensive positions inside the jungle. While Adler focused his NV glasses on the jungle beyond the river, Kalinin focused on the road leading to the mine.

Grant motioned Novak closer then whispered for him to set up inside the tree line, while he and Slade followed closely. The three cautiously wound their way through trees and brush, finally reaching the tree line. Between them and the water was thirty feet of open ground. Grant knew the mine was still seventy-five yards from their position. Just how many security guards were on duty, and what range those guards patrolled was unknown.

Novak chose a safe location inside the tree line, then adjusted the rifle's Starlight scope. Grant handed Slade the glasses, and first pointed toward the direction of the mine, then swept his arm sideways, signaling Slade to visually cover the area. Slade took cover near Novak, ensuring he was out of Novak's line of sight.

When both men were ready, Grant started forward, crouching low, then concentrating on the ground ahead, got on his belly and crabbed his way to the water's edge. He raised his NVGs before putting on a glove and removing the vial from his vest.

Water quickly filled the vial. Grant immediately pressed the rubber tip into the opening, but as he started crabbing his way backwards, he suddenly heard Novak in his earpiece, "Stop, boss; movement in trees across river." Grant went dead still. Novak zeroed in, then added, "Eyes on two, no, three males, civilian clothes, about your ten o'clock, weaving in and out of trees and obstacles. No weapons in sight yet. Wait. Point man has machete."

Grant silently questioned, *Who the hell are they? Where the hell did they come from?*

Holding his glasses with one hand, trying to spot the civilians, Adler pressed the PTT and whispered, "Doc, Vince, DJ, head 'em off, bring 'em here." Kalinin remained on defense.

Chapter 22

Grant stayed practically motionless, not even taking the chance of lowering his NVGs, but he smiled hearing Adler give the order, knowing it was exactly what he would've done. If luck was on their side, a G2 might be their best shot at learning whether the civilians knew anything about the Quds, and maybe even the hostages.

Staying inside the trees alongside the dirt road, Stalley, Milone and James ran south, then cut back and proceeded east across the narrow river.

Crouching low, they stepped onto the opposite bank, rushed into the trees, then immediately dropped to a knee, facing the last known direction reported by Novak.

Novak updated them. "They're at your twelve, moving quicker."

Adler zeroed on the civilians, then moved his glasses until locating his teammates. "Doc, they're about fifty yards from you, still at your twelve."

Knowing Adler had eyes on him, Stalley signaled with a thumb's up. But none of them were able to predict whether the civilians would suddenly change direction. Stalley backed up, concealing himself under large, green ferns, then motioned Milone to his nine o'clock. Milone crawled then took cover under a grouping of large drooping palm fronds about twenty feet from Stalley, who then signaled James to his three o'clock. James crawled the same distance, then backed up against the wide base of a palm tree. They were in position, listening for footsteps, or the chopping sound of a machete, and waiting for their teammates' updates.

In the meantime, Adler contacted Grant. "Skipper,

head toward me, slow and low."

Staying prone, Grant lowered his NVGs, then angled his body until he was able to begin crabbing his way toward the trees.

After he'd gone only several feet, he heard Adler, "You're in the clear."

Grant scrambled to his feet and bolted for the trees, quickly putting the vial and glove into his vest as he ran. Taking a knee next to Adler, he immediately pressed the PTT. "Mike, stay in position until civilians are in our hands. Ken, c'mon back."

Adler handed him his glasses, then whispered, "Look toward one o'clock."

Grant raised his NVGs, focused the glasses, then moved them slowly, finally spotting the three civilians, one behind the other, brushing aside drooping tree branches, large leaves, palm fronds that the machete failed to chop down. Moving the glasses farther right, Grant located his men, and pressed the PTT. "Civilians now about twenty yards from you; approaching from your twelve o'clock."

They heard the slashing of the machete, then gruff whispers, loud enough to understand that the civilians were speaking Spanish. Concentrating on the sounds, Stalley, Milone, and James held their silenced weapons across their bodies, as they looked right and left, preparing for the civilians to come from either side, but prepared to give chase.

The whispers and the slapping at palm fronds grew louder. Twigs and dried underbrush snapped beneath feet. Then, the point man walked between Stalley and

Milone, immediately followed by the next two men.

In loud, gruff whispers, and almost simultaneously, Milone, Stalley, and James ordered, "Alto! Alto!"

The civilians spun around, first spotting Milone, then Stalley, then James, as they walked from their concealed positions. Seeing black and green streaked faces, NVGs, plus weapons pointing directly at them, the civilians froze. The point man dropped the machete, just as the three fell to their knees, with their terrified voices starting to rise.

Stalley quickly stepped closer, continuously tapping a finger against his mouth, trying to quiet them. In the meantime, Milone and James had circled around the three, then shoved them face down onto the ground. With Stalley and Milone guarding the three, James withdrew zip-ties from his vest, tied hands behind backs, then one by one rolled each man onto his back, and slapped a strip of duct tape across his mouth.

Stalley backed away, and pressed the PTT. "Three secured; they're kids in their late teens. Over."

Teenagers?! Grant thought before responding, "Doesn't matter; get 'em here. Beat feet, Doc. Out."

Stalley, Milone, and James didn't waste another second. Jerking the captives to their feet, they each grabbed an arm, and, as Grant had directed, hustled to join their teammates.

Grant walked to the dirt road, and pressed the PTT. "Mike, do you have eyes on 'em yet?"

"Affirm."

"When they're close enough, set up near us. Copy?"

"Copy."

Grant glanced at his watch, then looked south along the road. "This is gonna have to be a fast G2," he mumbled.

"You've had enough practice," Adler remarked facetiously, while stepping next to him.

Ignoring the comment, Grant said, "I wanted to get into that mine before workers showed up."

"Sounds like you have more up your sleeve than just having a look."

They heard Novak in their earpieces, "On my way to you."

"There they are," Grant said, walking toward his men and the captives, pointing them toward the trees. Without even having to give an order to his men, they forced the three to the ground, making them sit with their backs to one another, forming a seated triangle. Stalley held up the machete for Grant to see.

Purposely keeping a hand on his holstered pistol, Grant stood briefly before each one, noticing disheveled brown hair, and sweaty faces. Pants and T-shirts were tattered and soiled, shoes were scruffy and covered in dust. But it was their expressions that impacted him, expressions showing obvious fear, and not only of him or his men. *These kids were on the run.*

He went near James, and whispered, "Did they have any bags or gear?"

James shook his head. "Only the machete."

Grant returned to the captives, and randomly selecting one, he squatted down, then slowly peeled off the duct tape. For a quiet moment he looked into brown eyes brimming with tears. Keeping his voice low, he finally asked, "English?"

"Sí, English," a shaky voice responded. "I speak little." A tear rolled onto his cheek, as he asked with surprise, "Americano?"

Grant nodded, then motioned for Adler to remove the duct tape from the other two before he drew his K-bar, sliced off the zip-tie, then handed the knife to Adler.

Grant asked in his limited Spanish, "Nombre?"

"Diego."

Grant motioned toward the other two. "Amigos?"

"Sí. Luís, Juan."

"Diego, were . you . running . away?"

"Run...ning? Oh, sí. Mucho."

"Why? Por qué?"

Diego was trying to find the right word. "A..fraid," he finally said, showing Grant his shaking hands.

Grant patted his shoulder, then motioned Milone closer. "Vince, try to get some answers. Ask if any of them have worked at the mine, have seen any prisoners, specifically, three men, one female, how many UFs he's noticed, and where he and his friends were heading."

While Milone was questioning, Grant motioned Adler closer, who asked, "Now what? Even if you get answers, this just might worsen our situation."

"Gimme the key for the van."

Adler dropped it in his hand. "You're actually giving them . . .?"

"It's the only way they'll have any kind of chance, Joe."

Milone quietly walked toward Grant and Adler, then reported, "Boss, those kids have been planning this for over a month. They did work the mine; but all the intel Diego had came second hand, reported by Juan's grandfather. He's been their lookout, per se. The only UFs were the ones guarding the mine, that is until two days ago when another five showed up. Those five left before dawn yesterday morning.

"You're not gonna like this, boss, but if I understood him correctly, the old man reported the UFs returned with two SUVs. If he counted correctly, seven people got out of the second one."

Shit! They're not at the mine! Grant remembered Simmons telling him any number of Iranians could've slipped into the country. Now he knew that as fact.

"He had one more detail, boss. A black SUV arrived yesterday morning. By early afternoon it was gone."

Grant arched an eyebrow. "How many were in it when it left?"

"Grandpa didn't know."

More and more unknowns, Grant worried.

Milone handed him a piece of note paper. "Diego drew this very rough diagram of the village. The X marks the house where all the UFs got out."

Grant looked briefly at the map. "Where were those three heading?"

"Some village five kilometers from here, where one of them has relatives. He estimated they'd walked a little over a kilometer to get here."

"Find out if any of them drive." A minute later Milone reported all three did.

"We've gotta stop wasting time," Grant said, as he took out a small notepad, quickly drew a map, then handed Adler the sat image and village map. "Joe, fill in the men while I try to explain the situation," he said, pointing toward the three young men.

Grant handed Diego the key and the map. With Milone helping to translate, Diego understood the directions to the property, location of the van, and once they were within two kilometers of their final destination, they were to abandon the van, ensuring it wouldn't be found.

Milone attempted to emphasize that they were never to mention the van, or what happened to them this morning. Only then did Stalley hand the machete to Juan.

Grant walked with the three to the dirt road, and pointed their way forward. He shook each of their hands, then motioned for them to move on, before he rejoined his men.

Adler handed him the simply-drawn diagram of the village, their objective. "It's impossible to know the actual size or number of buildings, but the X is where the hostages are supposedly being held, if everybody was telling the truth." He tapped the paper. "I think this is considered to be the main road. It's hard to say how far that X building is from the road and village."

Grant quickly perused the map, slipped it into his pocket, then looked toward the river. "We'll take the trail they just cleared. Ken, you're point again. It's about one klick to our objective, but we'll have to veer off that path when we've gone maybe three quarters of the way. Okay?" Slade nodded.

Grant adjusted his rucksack. "Let's move."

Chapter 23

Office of Director Ray Simmons
CIA
Langley
Sunday
0220 Hours - Local Time

A sudden loud rapping at the door woke Simmons from a brief, but deep, fifteen minute nap. He shook his head, and scrubbed a hand over his hair. "Yeah?"

Deputy Director Carl Gordon rushed in, then shoved the door closed. "Ray, here's an intel report and U-2 images sent over by the NRO. It isn't good." Gordon opened the folder and laid it on the desk.

Simmons rubbed his eyes, then went to his desk, put on his reading glasses, then, line by line, perused the one page report. "Oh fuck!"

"You said it. But now look at the images."

Simmons spread out three images. The first had a black line drawn with a Sharpie, marking the route of a multi-product pipeline starting in the northwest port of Santa Marta, near Medellin, then straight to Buenaventura. The second image had a black circle around Santa Marta and around Cartagena, where major refineries were located. The third image was split into three sections, all three enlarged and enhanced to show several groups positioned approximately three hundred yards away from the pipeline and based at various locations along its route.

"With the varying sizes and number of those groups,

Carl, there's only one explanation and conclusion. Not only are guerrilla groups involved in the Quds' operation, but I don't think we need much more proof that they're preparing to attack the pipeline in some way or other."

Gordon said, "The techs indicated another set of images was being scrutinized, which will show the coastline and refineries."

Simmons picked up the report. "Shit! There's nothing here indicating transmissions have been intercepted by us or NSA." Tossing the papers on the desk, his anger and frustration were exposed. "Dammit! Somehow Shahbaz was able to spread the word for them to prepare for this."

"It was all planned well ahead, Ray. You *know* that. They crossed all the t's and dotted all the i's, and all behind the scenes."

Simmons sat down heavily in his swivel chair. "I've gotta call Secretary McKinley. He'll make the decision on whether to notify the Israelis and Colombian authorities, although, I can't believe Colombia doesn't have a freakin' clue on what's going on."

"Do you think any of them are involved in the plan? They've either got a lot to lose *or* gain."

"Unknown, Carl. I'd better start calling everyone."

"Even the president?"

"Not yet. I'll ask for a meeting later in the morning."

"You know, Ray, we've only seen the images along *one* pipeline. Have you thought about the situation Captain Stevens and his men might be in, I mean, besides possibly facing a group of Iranians? What if . . .?"

"Carl, give me a suggestion, *any* suggestion on what

the hell I can do about it. We have no way to contact them without giving away their position. And we sure as hell can't send in a chopper." Gordon started to comment, until Simmons said with a regretful tone, "Maybe I shouldn't have called back the Gulfstream."

"You can't second guess, Ray. And besides, Captain Stevens and his men could've flown to the LHD when it transported the bodies. It was his decision to proceed."

Simmons laid a hand on the secure phone, but thought about the comments concerning the Colombian authorities. "Carl, have the techs review intercepts about four months back. See if anything was picked up from Colombian authorities who may have mentioned anything out of the ordinary concerning the pipelines. Then, check if those new images are ready, along with any new reports. I'll start making my calls."

Gordon had a hand on the door handle, but then turned toward Simmons. "Ray, maybe we should have NSA review some past transmission intercepts. There's also a possibility that flight transmissions were captured."

"Do it."

Chapter 24

Village of Aquilla
Sunday
0150 Hours Local Time

Team A.T. was keeping up a fast but cautious pace. *Three and a half hours till daylight,* Grant worried as he followed Slade along the beaten-down path. How long would it take before they found the objective, did a recon, then made their move? In what condition would they find the hostages? *Would* they find them?

Getting ready to leave the path, Slade shoved an arm out to the side, slowing everyone, then drew the machete from its sheath. He searched for any slight opening in the thick brush. Finding one, he veered off the path, then continued north toward the objective, with A.T. right behind him.

But compared to their pace along the worn trail, their current pace slowed dramatically. Instead of slashing at branches and fronds, Slade attempted to weave around, and push aside any obstacles in their path. Using his foot he cleared away twigs and small branches. Keeping sounds to a minimum was imperative.

Finally, he brought everyone to a stop, then motioned Grant next to him. They both took a knee, with the men following their lead. Twenty feet of jungle stood between them and the road leading into the village.

Signaling Slade, Grant grabbed his own wrist, as if a UF were being cuffed, then pointed ahead. Slade understood he was to watch for any UFs and signaled okay.

Adler crawled next to Grant, who pointed two fingers at his own eyes, then at Adler, then toward the right side of the village. Adler nodded, then crawling cautiously, he found a place that gave him a clear view along the rear of the buildings and property running north.

Grant raised his NVGs, then took out his glasses, first focusing on a crushed stone and dirt road coming from an easterly direction, before leading directly into a village that appeared to be in total disrepair. Built along both sides of the road were varied-sized structures, one- and two-stories, constructed of very worn, discolored vertical wood planks. Roofs, some peaked, some flat, were covered with plain or corrugated tin. Several of the flat roofs had lengths of wire rigged up as clotheslines. Clothes hung limply in the still, humid air. Parked at an angle near the end building was an old farm truck, its cargo bed framed on two sides with slated pieces of splintered wood. *That could come in handy,* Grant thought.

But then his mind turned to the civilians. How many were living and sleeping there? That was a major unknown, but there had to be enough who could work the mine every day. He gritted his teeth, picturing children carrying out the grueling task.

From his angle, every structure, whether home or otherwise, was completely dark. So far, no movement had been detected. He worried, *Could this also be where the Iranians who guard the mine crap out at night? But where? And how many are with the hostages? Damn!*

Lowering his NVGs, he took the village map from his pocket, and focused on the road drawn by Diego. He turned the map so it lined it up with the actual road, found the X, then looked in that direction. Putting the map away, he raised the NVGs, then focused his glasses on the dead end. Moving them slowly, he finally spotted a two-story house, built no more than forty yards beyond the village's west side. Lights shown from half open windows on the second story. Its one door was fully open. The first-floor door was also open, but its interior appeared to be dark. Along the left side of the house, chipped and cracked concrete stairs led to the second level deck. A wooden, slatted railing seemed to start at the back corner of the deck, then stretched across the entire front. *Was it a wraparound deck? Was there access from the rear of the house?*

He moved the glasses in order to see above the roof, as he looked for a power line. Spotting one on the north side, he followed it as it stretched from the front of the property to a tilted, wooden utility pole twenty yards from the house. The line drooped past the pole, disappeared briefly behind trees, then showed again attached to a pole close to the last building.

Grant sat back on his haunches, trying to visualize his next move. Was he to believe the young men's report that hostages were in that house? *No reason not to believe them,* he thought. But that was all he had to go on. That house had become the target.

Slade bumped an arm against him repeatedly, getting his attention, then pointed two fingers at his own eyes, then two at the target. Grant refocused the glasses, zeroing in on two men now standing outside the door on the second floor deck. They were both wearing dark green cammies. But the giveaway of who they were was that both had AK-47s hanging off straps hooked on their shoulders.

The right side of Grant's mouth curved up, as he thought, *Bingo!* But his smile soon disappeared, as he focused on the lower level. The door remained open. There was no way to be certain on which level the hostages were being held, but he opted for the top level.

He lowered the glasses briefly, looked toward the village, then raised the glasses again, moving them slowly as he scanned each building along the main road. Aside from worrying about how many UFs were guarding four hostages, he had just as much concern about the Iranians who guarded the mine. The Mossad reported there were five. *How many are currently at the mine? How many are in the village, and concealed in any one of those buildings, or maybe they're even inside the target?*

Just then, Adler moved closer to Grant and motioned him and the men farther back into the jungle. Once they were secured, Adler pointed at his two o'clock and whispered, "Behind those buildings, close to the trees, are two vehicles covered with camo netting. I wouldn't swear to it, but both look like the description of the agents' SUV. Do we need to check them out now?"

Grant shook his head. He realized finding a vehicle didn't necessarily mean the agents were still alive, but right now the house was their main objective. Getting back on track, his first decision was they'd use their Team call signs as often as possible. Next, he began laying out the plan.

Chapter 25

Remaining concealed within the trees, and using their glasses, Grant and Adler stayed focused on the target. Novak and Kalinin knelt between the two men, listening and watching for any movement in the village or along the road.

Grant whispered, "Clear." Adler was ready to keep eyes on Novak and Kalinin. Taking one last look along the road, Novak took the lead. Couching low, they darted from the trees, ran across the road, then headed for the rear of the buildings along the east side.

Adler kept them in sight, watching every movement as they slowly edged their way along the wooden structures, ducked under windows, until finally reaching the last building. They took a knee and sheltered in place, waiting.

Grant pressed the PTT, then barely whispered, "Seven-Three. Two UFs still on second deck. Stay low, you should be okay. Copy?"

Novak responded, "Copy." Novak looked over his shoulder at Kalinin, pointed to himself, then toward a small three-sided shed, shielding sacks of grain, some torn open, spilling their contents. Kalinin responded with a thumb's up, prepared to cover his teammate.

Novak leaned his head around the corner, took a final look, then hunching low, made a dash for the shed. Dropping to the ground, he crawled to the back corner. Then on his belly, he angled himself so he was head-on with the target. He opened the tripod attached to his rifle, adjusted the scope, then got comfortable.

Adler pressed the PTT, "Seven-Three is in position.

Kalinin was ready but waited for Grant's all clear, then finally heard, "Niner-Five, you're clear."

Within seconds, Kalinin was at the corner of the shed, immediately stretching out on his belly, ready to protect Novak and his other teammates. He and Novak were prepared to protect civilians if and when all hell broke loose. Flash-bangs against UFs were the grenades of choice. Tear gas canisters were to keep civilians away from the chaos. But if the civilians panicked, or if the UFs used them as human shields, instant, critical decisions would have to be made.

Adler reported, "Niner-Five is in position."

Grant motioned the rest of the Team closer to him while stashing his glasses. He, Stalley, and James would form one team. Adler, Slade, and Milone would form the other.

Grant pressed the PTT. "Seven-Three, can you see if deck wraps around north side?"

Novak replied, "Affirm, possibly extending across back. Over."

"Are we clear?"

"Two still outside; no longer using glasses. You're clear."

Grant motioned all his men forward. With Slade again in the lead, and staying within the jungle, they hustled past the village, watching for any irregularities, any lights, changes in the ground they ran across—anything. Low brush and palms gave them additional cover as they stopped to reexamine their position.

From Kalinin's angle he now could see his teammates. He pressed the PTT, contacting Grant. "Zero-

Niner. Niner-Five. Have you in sight. No additional lights; one UF on deck, second went inside."

Slade elbowed Grant, then pointed to tire tracks leading to the house, then across the front yard heading to the village. *A motorcycle,* Grant thought, as another thought raced through his mind. Was the motorcycle being used by a courier? Was this one of the ways messages and instructions were being passed around the country? *Is this the hideout for Shahbaz?! Shit! It's doubtful we'd be that lucky!*

The Team's remaining route to the target had already been established. Adler, Slade, and Milone were ready to head out first. Adler gave Grant a thumb's up, then the three men quickly headed for the trees and shrubbery lining the property behind the house. Once they were fifteen yards inside the tree line, they took a knee, then each scrutinized the entire rear of the building: no doors on either level; windows, halfway open; lights still visible on second level.

Knowing Grant had eyes on him, Adler motioned the three men toward him.

Cautiously moving forward, Grant was relieved to see a second set of concrete stairs leading from the right rear to the deck. *Something's gone right,* he thought. He pressed the PTT, then barely whispered, "Accessing deck from rear stairs; will proceed to back north corner. Out."

While Adler, Slade and Milone were waiting, Slade elbowed Adler's arm. Once he had Adler's attention, he cupped a hand around his own ear, indicating he heard voices, then pointed to the first floor. It was impossible to tell how many or what was being said. Adler silently cursed, wishing he had packed the shotgun mic. He always claimed it was powerful enough to detect a gnat's fart.

Once Grant, Stalley and James were nearby, Adler made the same hand cupping motion, then pointed to the lower floor. Grant signaled Adler to head toward the north side of the house.

Adler and his two men quietly walked through the brush, stopping in line with the north corner. Taking a final look, they cautiously walked across the property, then immediately backed up against the wood siding. Remaining under the deck, they slowly edged their way closer to the front corner.

From his angle near the shed, Novak only had eyes on the target and Adler. "Two-Seven. Seven-Three. Have eyes on. Lower outside is clear. Upper level has two UFs on deck; door closed." Something caught Novak's attention. "Both have glasses, appear to be looking toward road leading from village. Out."

One word went through eight minds: *Shit!*

Even though Kalinin could no longer see Grant, Grant was anticipating receiving the okay to proceed, especially with the UFs' attention now toward the road.

Finally he heard, "Zero-Niner. Niner-Five. Stay low, head to stairs—now."

Without hesitating, Grant, Stalley, and James raced from the trees toward the rear of the house , then took a knee. Slipping the straps of their MP5s over their heads, they swiveled the weapons behind their backs. James drew his suppressed Sig. Grant and Stalley left Sigs in place, but they each silently unsnapped the holster's restrainer, before drawing K-bars from leg straps.

Chapter 26

Kalinin saw Grant leaning slightly forward, pointing up and down with an index finger. Pressing the PTT, Kalinin notified everyone. "Zero-Niner moving into position on deck two. Clear."

With Grant in the lead, and keeping low, the three cautiously climbed the stairs. Grant stopped two steps before reaching the deck, then slowly straightened up. Seeing it was clear, he stepped onto the deck, then took cautious steps to the wall, pressed his back against it, then motioned Stalley toward him. The two sidestepped toward the first window, while James climbed onto the deck, taking his position at the back corner, ready to protect his teammates, prepared for any sudden appearance by a UF.

For a brief moment, Kalinin saw the three step onto the deck before they disappeared behind the house. He pressed the PTT, notifying Adler, "Two-Seven. Niner-Five. Three on deck."

Grant and Stalley slowly slid their backs down the siding, then hunching low, one by one they crept under the first window. The same discipline was followed for the next three windows. They could hear UFs inside speaking in Farsi.

Kalinin updated them twice, indicating the UFs at the front were near the door.

Reaching the back north corner, Grant took a breath then leaned his head slightly, expecting Novak to catch sight of him.

Novak had his scope zeroed in on the north side deck, prepared to give the signal for the next maneuver. With his rifle barrel balanced on the tripod, he kept his right hand just outside the trigger guard, as he used his left to press the PTT, contacting Adler. "Two-Seven. Zero-Niner is in position. On my mark: three, two, one. Go."

Adler took a step out from under the deck, pulled the pin, and immediately threw the smoke grenade high above the electrical power line. Red smoke immediately started swirling into the air, the opaque smoke's width expanding even before the canister hit the ground. As it rolled, thick smoke continued belching from the canister.

Adler quickly backed up against the wall near his men, slowly edging his way toward the front corner. He leaned just enough to see that the area leading across the front of the house was clear.

On the upper deck, Bijan Akbari spotted the mass of swirling smoke that appeared out of nowhere. He grabbed Vahid Mazdaki's arm, pointed, then began running toward the northeast corner, keeping one hand on his holstered pistol, the other holding his glasses.

Mazdaki paused by the open doorway, and ordered in Farsi, "Shut the door! Stay inside until I give the all clear!" He leaned over the railing, gave the same order to the men downstairs, then took off, catching up to Akbari. Two doors slammed shut, then sudden, simultaneous sounds emanated from rooms on both levels—the clicking sounds of rifle bolts.

Mazdaki looked overhead, his eyes briefly settling on the electrical wire that was still intact. He raised his glasses. Both men focused on the thick, swirling red smoke, trying to see beyond it, through it, around it, looking for any movement.

The Team heard Kalinin in their earpieces, "Two UFs on deck, northeast corner; lower level clear."

Grant saw the UFs, then waved Stalley forward. They had to act while the UFs were distracted. Staying close to the wall, they moved quickly. Not hearing any other warning from either Novak or Kalinin, the two made their move.

Chapter 27

As the smoke began dissipating, Akbari spotted the canister, and pointing in its direction, shouted, "Look! Over there!"

Grant and Stalley were behind the two in a heartbeat, reaching around, slapping hands across mouths, and violently jerking heads back. With a single, fluid motion, K-bars sliced through carotids. Blood spurted.

Keeping their hands across the UFs' mouths, Grant and Stalley wasted no time and dragged the collapsing men backwards, out of view. Then kneeling, they continued applying pressure against the mouths. The UFs' eyes were wide open, blood continued flowing from the wounds, pooling on the deck. Their bodies spasmed. Suddenly, their eyes rolled back, bodies went limp. Only then did Grant and Stalley release them, the entire event taking just under thirty seconds.

Novak notified the Team. "Two UFs down. Hold positions."

In rapid succession, Grant and Stalley slid K-bars into leg straps, quickly wiped bloody hands on their cammies, then drew their Sigs. They stepped around the bodies, plastering their backs against the wall, while holding weapons with both hands, close to their chests.

Voices began shouting in Farsi, with someone finally calling, "Bijan!" Silence. And then, "Vahid!" Responses were nonexistent. The shouts gradually subsided, but as concerned as they were, the Iranians stayed inside as ordered.

Arash Imani nervously paced back and forth across

the wood floor, occasionally looking toward the front door, tempted to go out on deck. But he knew to heed Mazdaki's warning to remain inside until the all clear was given.

"What are we waiting for?" Roshan Jafari queried angrily.

"They must be searching the property. We must wait!" Imani replied emphatically. "We do not even know what caused the warning from Vahid!" He waved an arm overhead. "He and Bijan have . . .!"

"They have had more than enough time!" Kenan Habib interrupted. "We should be involved! It is time!"

It only took Imani three steps to be standing toe to toe with Habib. Jamming a finger constantly against Habib's chest, Imani warned, "Perhaps I should send you out— alone."

Habib slapped Imani's hand away. "Save your threats for somebody else, Arash!"

Inside the first floor main room, and listening to the unsettling argument going on above them, were three Iranians, also members of the Quds Force. But they had not been involved in the attack on the Israelis and Americans. They were part of the mine's security team, and when daylight arrived, they were scheduled to relieve the men on duty. But whatever caused the urgency, they were prepared to assist their brethren. With AKs in hand, they took defensive positions next to windows, waiting for further orders.

Grant, Stalley, and James were ready to take action, but remained cautious, not knowing if the hostages were inside, and if they were, whether the suspicious UFs would use them as human shields. But this could be the chance to get any UFs out into the open.

Enough! Grant thought. It was time to locate the hostages. He turned, pointed at Stalley, then drew an outline of a small square, before pointing to the rear of the house. Stalley nodded, then quietly headed for the rear, prepared to look in windows.

On the first level, Adler and his men were ready for confrontation. But the main question was who, and how many would they be confronting? As it stood right now, they had to be prepared for anything, ready to use their next option, even though it wasn't the safest.

They began hearing hurried footsteps, and muffled, anxious voices from inside the rooms, but the only words understood were the mentioning of the same two names: Bijan and Vahid.

While Novak was keeping eyes on the target and his teammates, Kalinin scooted behind the corner of the shed, using his glasses to look toward the village. No civilians were in sight, nor were there any lights. And except for some louder than normal voices at the target, there wasn't anything suspicious for the civilians to investigate, unless their fear of retribution by the UFs prevented any curiosity.

Kalinin was very aware that the silence around him could all change in a heartbeat. He repositioned himself where he had a clear view of the target, then removed a canister of tear gas from his vest, placing it within easy reach.

Grant decided he had to chance it and use the PTT.

Stepping farther away from the corner, he pressed the button. Barely whispering, he contacted Kalinin. "Niner-Five. Any lights, movement in village?"

"Negative."

Just as Grant was ready to contact James, out of the corner of his eye he saw Stalley motioning him to the rear. Barely whispering, Stalley reported, "Three hostages, bound, gagged, at second window, eyes on me."

Grant smiled and gave a thumb's up, before thinking, *Experience should warn them to prepare for shit to happen.* But then another question struck him and he whispered, "Woman?" Stalley shook his head, and signaled with a thumb's down.

Grant wondered, *Where the fuck have they stashed her? First floor? The jungle?!* He had to wipe the thought from his brain that she may have suffered abuse, because right now he had to concentrate.

He signaled Stalley to stand watch near the front corner, while he moved back. He had to advise his men, and immediately pressed the PTT, whispering, "Three male agents alive, second floor, right rear. Hold positions."

Adler understood that the order to "hold positions" was meant mostly for him and his two men. Grant didn't want them beginning a search for the Mossad agent, at least, not yet. But Adler silently questioned, *Where the hell is she?*

Grant's mind raced. *It's gonna be daylight before we know it.* It was time to take drastic measures.

Chapter 28

Having no idea what the UFs were prepared to do, Grant had to quickly devise a new plan. He pressed the PTT, quietly contacting James. "Six-Eight. Zero-Niner. Need you here."

James backed away from the southeast corner, then hunching under windows, he hurried to Grant's position.

Grant scribbled a short note, showed it to James, then handed it to Stalley. While Stalley read the order, Grant wrote another, this one printed in large letters. Stalley understood both notes, then took off toward the rear.

Grant had one more brief note to pass on. Completing it, he held it up for Novak to see, pointed down toward Adler's position, then held the note over the railing.

Novak whispered into his throat mic, contacting Adler, "Two-Seven. Zero-Niner is prepared to drop paper to you."

Surprised, Adler stepped away from the overhang. As soon as Adler came into view, Grant dropped the folded paper. Adler grabbed it as it floated down, read it, signaled Grant with a thumb's up, then showed the note to Slade and Milone, before removing a flash-bang from his vest.

Finally, Grant held a flash-bang for Novak to see, then pointed down toward Adler's position. Novak whispered into his throat mic, "A.T. Zero-Niner and Two-Seven ready with flash-bangs." Hearing those two words, Team A.T. ensured earplugs were in place.

Stalley was at the second window, listening for voices. The UFs had gone silent, presumably expecting instructions. Leaning his head slightly, Stalley looked in the room ensuring no UFs were present, while noticing the door was partially open.

He tapped on the raised window, and got the agents' attention, while trying to keeping an eye out for UFs who could suddenly come busting into the dark room. He held the printed note so the agents could read the words: FLASH-BANGS! The three men bobbed their heads, then watched Stalley hold up his MP5, then point down near where he was standing. Understanding the message, they scooted backwards on their butts, placing their bodies against a wall, then drew their knees in, lowered their heads and closed their eyes. With wrists tied behind their backs, there was nothing they could do to deaden the up-coming sound.

Stalley crumbled the note and jammed it in a pocket. Getting down on a knee below the window, he set his MP5 to semi-auto, then waited.

James had already received his instructions, the final order that Grant would give before all hell broke loose.

Chapter 29

Novak saw that Grant was ready with the grenade, and contacted Kalinin. "Niner-Five. Get ready for flash-bang toss. Copy?"

"Copy." Kalinin first shot a quick glance at the tear gas canister, mentally picturing its location if and when he had to grab it. Then he closed his eyes and lowered his head.

Standing near the front corner, holding the flash-bang in one hand, with the other hand ready to pull the pin, Grant nodded at James.

James cupped both hands around his mouth, then in Farsi, he began shouting, sounding more frantic with each continuous call. "HELP! HELP ME! HELP ME!"

A wave of alarm, and sudden commotion erupted on both the first and second levels. Imani pointed toward Habib and ordered, "Guard the prisoners!" Habib ran toward the back bedroom, and posted himself next to the partially open door.

Front doors flung open. Imani was the first one out, with Jafari on his heels, both turning in all directions, trying to locate either Akbari or Mazdaki. "Vahid!" Imani shouted.

On the first level, the three Iranians ran out, one behind the other, aiming their weapons, as they looked at every angle of the property, listening for further cries for help.

For the UFs on both levels, the sound of an object landing near them gave them little time to react before a five million candlepower, blinding flash of light, and a thunderous, earsplitting sound immediately triggered a temporary loss of vision, and ringing in their ears. Groaning in pain, they pressed their hands against their ears, squeezed their eyes shut. Their vision began clearing in twelve seconds, but their sense of balance was totally disrupted. They stumbled around helplessly, bumping into one another. Two men on the first level fell to their knees.

From his location in the house, Habib wasn't affected by the blast as severely as the others, except for slightly blurred vision and incessant ringing in his ears. Unsteadily, he started toward the front door, then remembering Imani's order, he staggered back toward the bedroom. He kicked the partially open bedroom door, nearly losing his balance. With his vision remaining blurry, he blinked continuously, trying to locate the three agents inside the dark room, aiming his rifle in every direction.

His reaction to a sudden, blurred movement near a back window, and a weapon pointing through the opening was a millisecond before consecutive rounds penetrated his body at center mass, knocking him off his feet. His body impacted the wood floor with a loud, deep-sounding *thud,* a half second before his head struck the wood. Blood drained from two chest wounds, rapidly spreading across his dark green shirt, pooling under his body.

Stalley continued focusing on and aiming his weapon at the body. With a loud, gruff whisper, he said to the agents, "Stay down! Stay down!" The three rolled onto their sides, curling up to make themselves smaller targets, if it came to that.

Stalley pressed the PTT. "Five-Two reporting three

agents safe; one UF eliminated." No response was expected.

Grant and James had cautiously rounded the corner, taking slow deliberate steps, aiming their silenced Sigs toward the confused, in pain Iranians. James, leaning close to the railing in order for the UFs on the first floor to hear him, began shouting in Farsi, ordering, "Toss your weapons! On your knees! On your knees! Hands behind your heads! Do it!"

Having been so close to the blast, the Iranians' loss of vision and hearing was taking longer to clear. The voice that was shouting orders in their language seemed distant, choppy, unclear. The images moving closer were blurred.

James ordered again, "Get . on . your . knees!"

Finally, the words penetrated the Iranians' brains. Jafari squinted, attempting to bring the moving, blurred images into focus. Once he obeyed the order, he angrily questioned in Farsi, "Who are you?!" No response.

Imani knelt slowly, and as he was going down, he reached for his pistol, had it halfway out of the holster, when Grant fired two rapid rounds, both rounds causing massive hemorrhaging. Imani collapsed in a bloody heap.

Jafari fell back in total shock. While Grant kept his weapon aimed, James hurried behind Jafari and shoved him face forward onto the deck, then zip-tied his arms behind his back.

Once the Iranian was secured, Grant walked near James, and whispering, ordered him to take the prisoner to Adler.

Grant entered the room cautiously, not knowing how many Iranians could've been involved. Holding his Sig with both hands, he scanned the main room, then went to the first bedroom, lowered his NVGs, then shoved the door hard enough that it hit the wall. He stepped in, immediately looked left, then continued scanning the room, past the two windows, when he suddenly stopped. In the corner was a stockpile of Uzis, *Desert Eagles* and Glocks, holsters, rifle straps, a sniper rifle, magazines for pistols and Uzis, a canvas bag, four leather satchels. *Jackpot!* He knelt near the bag, quickly examined the contents, noticing another Glock. *Weapons accounted for,* he thought, before checking each satchel, finding in one a small hard case, slightly larger than a cigarette pack. Inside he found an empty glass vial on black foam. He put the case in his vest, then as he left the room, it dawned on him that he counted five Glocks. *Five?*

He slid his pistol into the holster. Turning his attention to the deck, he dragged Jafari's body inside. As he headed toward the bedroom, several objects on a wooden table got his attention: two walkie talkies, a radio, sat phone, and a GPS. *Make that two,* he silently thought, seeing another GPS poking out from under a pile of white cloths.

"Uh-oh," he quietly said, focusing on the radio and sat phone. Were the Iranians able to discover the frequencies and secure numbers the agents used? The odds were probably against them, but still . . .

Confident that the Team's call signs were no longer needed, he reverted to names, then continually held down the PTT for his next few conversations. "Joe, are your prisoners secured?"

"Three secured."

"Any sign of the woman?"

"Only that she must've been here, 'cause I found a web belt, a pair of black women's jeans and a shirt." Silence. "Skipper?"

"I heard you, Joe. Just leave them for now. We'll put them inside the canvas bag."

"Want me to start a G2?"

"Affirm, but do it inside. They're all supposed to be fluent in English. DJ can assist if they break into Farsi. I'm on my way to talk with agents. Nick, any lights or movement in village?"

"A couple of lights, no movement yet, but they *must've* heard the gunfire and blasts."

Grant glanced at his watch. "Time's approaching for them to start work at the mine. We may have to prevent that. Stay ready. Mike, reposition near Nick. Copy?"

"Copy."

"Doc, I'm ready to enter; remain on defense for now. Copy?"

"Copy."

Taking the radio and sat phone with him, Grant stepped into the room, seeing Stalley through the window, facing toward the property. Grant walked toward Habib's body, trying to avoid stepping in a puddle of blood. He squatted down behind Habib's head, then placed two fingers near the windpipe, checking for a pulse. He didn't expect to find one, but it was one of those determinations he'd enter into his AAR (After Action Report).

As he stood, he noticed the agents near the opposite wall, still continuing to follow Stalley's order to stay down. Walking closer, he raised his NVGs, then quietly said, "It's over, gentlemen. You're safe now."

Chapter 30

Grant laid the radio and sat phone on the floor. Then one by one, he helped the agents sit up. Even in the dark, the injuries became apparent, along with exhaustion, hunger and dehydration. He immediately noticed dried blood on the side of Jacobs' face. He called out, "Doc, need you here."

Grant removed the strip of cloth covering Jacob's mouth. The agent licked his dried, cracked lips, then tried to smile as he offered his hand. "Sam Jacobs. And you are?"

"Grant Stevens, sir." Grant sliced through the wrist restraint with his K-bar. "Sorry we couldn't get here sooner. But rest assured, you'll all be outta here soon. There's an LHD waiting off the coast ready to send choppers."

Stalley rushed into the room, and immediately went near Grant, who pointed toward Jacobs. "Doc, take a look at Agent Jacobs first." Stalley knelt next to the agent, handing him a canteen. Quickly evaluating the wound, Stalley immediately opened his medical bag.

Grant was untying the cloth from Salzman's mouth when he noticed a dark swelling around the agent's eye, and bruise on his cheekbone. He commented with a quick smile, "That's quite a shiner you've got, sir."

"I was lucky," Salzman replied as he looked toward Beatty. "You need to check Clint. He took a rifle butt to the back of his head."

"Doc will handle it, sir," Grant said. He cut through Salzman's restraints, then gave him a canteen. "Drink up."

Salzman took a long swig, then offered a hand to Grant. "Joel Salzman." He tried to stand, but his legs gave out almost immediately.

"Whoa!" Grant said, helping him sit. "You need to take it easy." Grant pressed the PTT. "Ken, need your canteen."

"On my way."

Grant crawled closer to Beatty, removed the cloth, cut the restraints, then patted Beatty's shoulder. "You'll be okay, sir."

"Here's ya go, boss," Slade said, handing the canteen to Grant. Grant passed it to Beatty, then motioned Slade to the side. Keeping his voice low, he asked, "How's the G2?"

"Like pulling teeth, but we found out the three Iranians downstairs worked at the mine. Two more are already there on security detail."

Grant crossed his arms over his chest, as he lowered his head. "Which means it was the other five who perpetrated the attack." His eyes met Slade's. "I take it Neman wasn't mentioned?"

Slade shook his head. "Nobody's given up anything on her."

"Okay, Ken. Tell Joe to use *any* means necessary to drag out that intel." Slade started to leave when Grant added, "Ken, there are two bodies on the north side deck. Put them in the main room, then check for keys in their pockets and the pockets of that guy," he said, pointing to Imani's body.

Slade left. Just then, Kalinin reported, "There's activity in the village; civilians heading toward the farm vehicle."

"Okay, Nick. Vince, need you to meet up with Nick and Mike, then somehow you've gotta explain to those civilians that they *cannot* go to the mine. It'd be best if they remained indoors. They'll be safe if they follow instructions. Copy?"

"Copy, boss. Want me to give them a quick explanation on the Iranians?"

"Very brief, but before you leave, have DJ ready the sat phone for contacting the LHD, then bring it to me."

"Roger. Uh, boss, you know the three young men . . .?"

"If anyone starts to panic when they discover they're missing, just tell them that they're safe. The less they know, the better—for all parties."

"Copy that."

Grant didn't have a sliver of doubt that he and his men had to get to the mine and eliminate the two Iranians on watch. Destroying the weapons was a necessity, even knowing the gold could be a means for the civilians' survival. He had to contact Simmons. Decisions had to be made without delay.

Chapter 31

While he waited, Grant returned to the agents, then took a knee in front of Salzman. But before he could question him, Salzman asked, "What the hell happened to the Mossad team?"

"Three of them were killed."

"Oh, fuck," Salzman mumbled, dropping his head back. But then, he looked again at Grant. "Wait! Three? There were supposed to be four at that meeting!"

"Did you see four when you arrived?"

Salzman shook his head. "No. Clint was in contact with Neman, who had given us the all clear to proceed to the house. We saw her in the doorway when we pulled up."

"Sorry, sir, but we only found three males."

Salzman's surprised look immediately worried Grant, especially after Salzman asked, "You mean you haven't found her here, or anywhere?"

"No, sir."

"I told you when we last saw her." Salzman looked overhead as if in thought. "She *was* in the doorway." He turned toward Beatty. "Clint, didn't you say you had eyes on someone behind her?"

"I did. One male, but he moved out of sight as we got closer."

That had to be an Iranian, Grant thought.

Salzman continued, "We'd just gotten out of the vehicle when the attack began. I didn't see her after that. Once the firefight ended, we were blindfolded. What I do remember was one of the Iranians ordering that we all be put in our vehicle, and he also ordered that the others return to *their* vehicle. We all ended up here. Dammit! What'd they do with her?"

"I wish I could answer that, sir."

Beatty gingerly rested his head against the wall, and keeping his eyes closed, said, "I guess you know Agent Kaufman was killed."

"Yes, sir. His body was in the house. We called in a chopper. His and the Mossad men's bodies were transported to it. I don't know what other arrangements were worked out."

"Well, thank you for taking care of him . . . them."

"Our pleasure, sir."

Stalley tapped his shoulder. "Let me take look at him." Grant back away.

Several minutes later, Stalley motioned Grant toward the center of the room, then quietly reported, "I used butterflies instead of stitches on Agent Jacob's wound. The bleeding stopped, but he might be needing additional work. His cheekbone might have a hairline crack. Agent Beatty has a mild concussion, but otherwise, he checked out. Salzman checked out okay, considering. I gave all of them Tylenol. They'll get a thorough exam in sickbay."

"Okay, Doc. Listen, take pictures of the bodies, and the live ones. You can take some of the village on our way out." Stalley grabbed his bag, then left.

Grant returned to the agents, then took a knee in front of them. "I found a stockpile of weapons in the other room, Uzis, Mini-Uzis, *Desert Eagles,* Glocks, and a sniper rifle."

"We had the folding stock Uzis and the Glocks," Jacobs confirmed.

"No sniper rifle?"

"No."

"So that means the other weapons belonged to the Israelis."

"Sounds right," Salzman confirmed.

"And the leather satchels were yours?" Salzman nodded. Grant stood, and slid his hands into his pants' pockets. "If we've already accounted for three dead Israelis, then why are there four Mini-Uzis, three *Desert Eagles* and one Glock in that stockpile?"

"Oh, Christ," Salzman mumbled. "The extras were Neman's. We'd been informed that she always carried a Glock."

"That's what I suspected. But it still doesn't give us any clue where she is."

Beatty said, "Remember, the Iranians had their own vehicle. If it's not on the property, that means someone could've driven it and her outta here."

"Did any of you hear an engine start?" Grant asked.

The three men shook their heads, then Jacobs said, "But that doesn't mean anything."

"Sirs, I don't think anyone should jump to conclusions right now." Grant remembered the young men mentioning another SUV arrived and departed yesterday, but decided to keep it to himself.

A quiet moment passed before Grant added, "My men are trying to get answers from the prisoners." He let his eyes go to each agent, then asked, "Do you think you could identify the ones who attacked you?"

"Maybe not all of them, but sure," Salzman answered, with Beatty and Jacobs giving the same response.

"Good." Grant reached into his vest, took out the small, hard case, along with the water-filled vial, handing both to Salzman. "Director Simmons asked that I get a sample of the water, just in case you were unable to, sir."

"Appreciate that."

Grant pointed down to the GPS units, radio and sat phone. "Can I assume those are yours?"

Salzman swallowed a mouthful of water, then picked up the sat phone. "Yeah, they're ours."

"The frequencies were set before we departed D.C.," Beatty commented while lightly laying a hand on the battle dressing.

Novak's voice sounded in Grant's earpiece. "Boss, no other villagers have showed up."

"Okay. Stay with Nick and Vince."

"Roger."

Grant released the button for a couple of seconds, then contacted Adler. "Joe, check the Iranians for vehicle keys." Without waiting for a reply, he released the button.

Slade walked next to him, holding out a hand, palm up. "They're similar, boss."

Grant reached for the two keys, as he heard Adler, "Skipper, found a key on one of the mine security guys. It's for the truck."

"Wait one, Joe." Grant showed the keys to the agents. "Can you identify either as the Nissan's?"

"Hard do say," Beatty replied. "Pete did all the driving."

"Okay. Joe, Ken found two keys. He's on his way to the vehicles." As Slade was about to leave, Grant said, "Ken, pick up the smoke canister down the hill. It should be at the eleven o'clock position." Slade left. Holding down the PTT button, Grant said, "Everybody needs to stand-by if the situation gets outta hand with the civilians. We can't let them go to the mine."

"Understood," Adler replied. "Have you mentioned the found clothes to the agents?"

"About to. Listen. Doc's got things under control here. I'll contact the LHD, then try for Simmons."

"What's gonna happen to the Iranians, both dead and alive?"

"TBD (to be determined), Joe. That might be up to Simmons. I'm gonna make the call." Grant turned toward the agents, lowered his head for a moment, then his eyes went to each man before he finally said, "I held off telling you in case we got new intel, but a black web belt, a woman's pair of jeans, and a shirt were found in a room downstairs."

"Sonofabitch!"

Simultaneously, Beatty and Jacobs let loose. "Dammit! Dammit!"

There wasn't much Grant could add, except, "Sirs, I'm sorry, but I don't expect we're gonna have time to search any further for . . ."

Salzman interrupted, "Stop! Don't even go there. You've gone above and beyond already. Okay?"

Grant' smile was brief, then he held up his sat phone. "I'm gonna order your ride. It should take under thirty minutes for the chopper to arrive."

"Did I hear you say that you're gonna call Director Simmons?" Salzman asked.

"Yes, sir. I've gotta update him on a few urgent matters, and confirm whether or not our mission's been extended—again."

"While you do that, I can contact the DDO (Deputy Director for Operations) using our sat phone."

"Sir, I'd like to suggest that you hold off until you're aboard the LHD. You'll probably have a lengthy conversation, so it might be best if you use the ship's communication equipment. I'll be certain to pass the word to the director that you're all safe."

"Understood, but," Salzman began with his brow furrowing, "how do *you* plan on . . .?"

"Maybe we can discuss that another time."

"I'll be waiting with bated breath."

The right side of Grant's mouth curved up, as he was removing a few Snickers bars from his vest. He handed them toward the men. "That might tide you over till you chow down aboard the ship."

"Excellent!" Salzman said, licking his chops.

"Look, while I go make my call, and if any of you feel able, why don't you get your weapons and gear? While you're at it, you may as well collect the Israelis' gear. You can stow everything aboard the chopper."

"Good idea," Jacobs replied, helping Beatty stand. "But what about the Iranians' weapons?"

"TBD, sir."

"What are you gonna do with them, I mean the Iranians?"

"TBD, sir."

Grant offered a hand to Salzman, helping him stand, then waited until the three men were steady on their feet. "Okay, gentlemen, follow me. The gear's in the second bedroom."

As Grant stepped outside, he picked up the flash-bang canister, then walked to the northeast side of the deck. After checking the coordinates using the GPS, he pressed the PTT. "A.T., I'm preparing to contact *Iron-clad*, so stand-by."

"Boss," Slade interrupted, "the keys fit the Nissans."

"Copy that, Ken. C'mon back." Now the Team had use of both Nissans and the truck. Time would tell whether any would come into play. He pressed the green button on the sat phone, then entered a string of numbers.

Chapter 32

Radio Room
USS *Roeti Island*

First Class Petty Officer Bob Artis sat at the console, eyeing a new package of cheese and peanut butter crackers. He stripped off the cellophane, took one from the package, and as he was ready to pop it into his mouth, the sat phone assigned to the current mission sounded. He answered, "*Ironclad*."

"*Ironclad*, this is Tango 8."

"Go ahead, Tango 8." Hearing the call sign Tango 8, Artis' supervisor stepped next to him.

Grant proceeded, "Request that you advise Condor 1 and Condor 2 that they are to stand-by for upcoming orders. Advise them there will be civilians in the vicinity of their objective. Here are the objective's coordinates." Grant relayed the numbers, then requested, "Repeat those coordinates, *Ironclad*." Artis did as requested, then Grant said, "I'll advise later when Condor 1 and 2 are to depart from *Ironclad*. I'm requesting now that you patch me through to Langley. You can use the main number; I'll take it from there."

"Understood. Wait one." Artis located CIA's main number, and as he was entering the numbers, he asked, "Anything else, Tango 8?"

"Negative. Thanks, *Ironclad*."

Artis disconnected, then, as ordered, he immediately revealed all details to his supervisor.

*

CIA
Langley

The main phone at Langley rang once. The agent on duty answered, "00628973257."

Grant responded with a two-part code, the first was for Simmons, the next was his. "34732867 - 324538."

"Hold on."

The director's phone rang twice. "Simmons."

"Sir, it's Grant."

Simmons got Gordon's attention, set the phone to scramble, then pressed the speaker button. "Captain, I've got you on speaker. Carl Gordon's with me. Go ahead."

"As an FYI, sir, my call's being patched through by the radio room on *Ironclad*. There may be some inter-ruption of service because of our location."

"Understood."

"Sir, there's a lot to report, but not enough time to re-lay all the details, but I'll do my best." Simmons under-stood that to mean: don't interrupt me. Grant continued, "I know that Agent Nyland updated you on Agent Kauf-man, but we found your other three agents alive, sir, in Aquilla, our current location."

Simmons quietly said, "Thank God."

"Doc handled their minor injuries, but they'll report to sickbay once aboard *Ironclad*. We haven't found the Mossad woman, Ashira Neman. There's evidence, though, that she was taken from the meeting place by the Iranians and transported here to Aquilla. I've made the decision to discontinue searching for her, sir, unless you or the Israelis decide otherwise.

"Here are a couple of side notes. First, your men indicated the Iranians had their own vehicle. We found it on this property. Next, I turned over a water-filled vial to Agent Salzman. The agents are in possession of their weapons and gear. We'll collect the Iranians' gear and weapons."

Both Simmons and Gordon were rapidly taking notes, readying questions, listening as Grant continued, "We've got four Iranian prisoners, four others are dead. We're certain three of those that are still alive were security for the mine. If intel was correct, there are two more on guard at the mine, and due to be relieved around 0600.

"Now, as far as the others, we're certain they're the ones who pulled off the ambush at the meeting location. If you've lost count, sir, four of *them* are dead.

"When we're finished here, and if you approve, I'll call for the chopper, or choppers. One or two will depend on whether we're ordered to accompany the Iranians and the agents to the LHD. What happens to the Iranian bodies must also be decided. You may not want that to be my decision, sir, but I'd be willing to make it because the fridge aboard the LHD could get mighty full."

Simmons replied, "I agree, Captain." He whispered to Gordon to call Secretary McKinley, then said to Grant, "Captain, Carl's going to contact Secretary McKinley, who will review this with the Israelis. I hope to have an answer before this call ends."

"Very well. Sir, all this could also change if you authorize me to proceed with the mission and see it through to its fruition. I'd like to check out the mine, and ensure that it'll no longer be useful or profitable to the Iranians.

"One last item is that Doc took pictures at both locations, which should be more than enough to tell the story, sir.

"I think that's all. I'm ready for your questions."

Simmons rocked his chair back and forth, while tapping his pen on the notepad. "Captain, first let me thank you and your men for finding our men."

"Our pleasure, sir. We're glad it turned out the way it did."

A brief moment of silence ensued, until Simmons said, "I know you'll be writing up an AAR, but fill me in on a couple of things. First, what's your true opinion on what happened to Neman?"

"Not good, sir. The last time the agents saw her was at the meeting place. Her weapons and gear were found in the house at our present location. Also, a web belt, a woman's pair of jeans, and a shirt were found in this house. We're putting those in the canvas bag we believe was hers and will have it and the weapons transported to the LHD. Other than that, there's been no trace of her."

"I see. For now, I think you gave me enough information on the Iranians. What I'd like to know is why you don't think your mission is over? Finding our men *was* your mission."

"There are two more Iranians at that mine that need to be dealt with, sir."

"Is your plan to also transport them to the LHD along with the others?"

"That's . . . highly doubtful, sir. But beyond that is-sue, we'll be able to confirm whether there are weapons stashed inside as suspected. An, sir, I see no reason for Tehran to profit from the gold. On this property there's a section that appears to have been for planting crops. The ground hasn't been turned over for quite some time. That was the villagers main way of life. They produced a good portion of their sustenance, until the Iranians showed up. Sir, if we find any gold, do we have permis-sion to turn it over to the civilians?"

"All right, Captain. Look, I'll authorize your request concerning the mine, but what about your extraction, and the number of choppers you'll . . .?"

"One should be enough to transport the Iranians and your men, sir. I'll call in the other chopper once we've completed our work."

"And you have the means to carry out the . . . work?"

"That's affirmative, sir. We never leave home without the required items."

Chapter 33

After a brief pause in the conversation, Simmons finally said, "If you have an extra minute or two, I have some pertinent intel. At 0215 this morning, we received U-2 images that showed activity along a pipeline. By activity I mean, varied-sized groups were spotted at different locations. The total number of groups and each size would indicate the guerrillas have joined in the Quds' operation. I'm waiting for the NRO to send over more recent images that might tell us more."

"So, the Iranians' plan has begun."

"It appears so."

"Sir, does the pipeline run anywhere near our current location or the mine?"

"Don't even *think* about it, Captain."

Grant warned himself, *Hold your tongue, Stevens.* "Sir, I was only wondering if that *were* the case, would the guerrillas or Quds pose any danger to the village or even us before we can get outta here, considering the method we'll use to complete our work?"

"Oh, I see. Well, they appear to be posted at block valve and pump stations only. Hold on." Simmons shuffled through several papers. "The closest stations are at least fifteen to twenty miles to your East and Southeast. The pipeline ends at Buenaventura."

"We should be all right then."

Simmons noticed his office door opening. Carl Gordon rushed in. Leaving the speaker on, Simmons said, "Captain, hold on." As Gordon laid a sheet of paper on the desk, Simmons asked Gordon, "Any response from Secretary McKinley?"

"No. But, Ray, look at that paper. We may have finally gotten some sorta break." Simmons spun the paper around, as he lowered his reading glasses. Gordon pointed at the paper. "That transmission was intercepted coming outta Buenaventura, and it wasn't from personnel working at the port."

Grant silently questioned, *When's the Al Sham due to dock? Tomorrow!*

Simmons continued reading, then finally said, "Captain, the transmission was from a sat phone. A male voice, speaking in Farsi, contacted the captain of the *Al Sham*. He requested an update on her arrival in Buenaventura. According to the captain, she'll arrive ahead of schedule at 1900 tonight. But because harbor pilots end work at sunset, port authority personnel advised he wouldn't be able to dock. He was directed to drop anchor in the harbor until 0600 Monday when the harbor pilots start work."

"Sir," Grant began, "what was so important that contact had to be made? I mean, all they're expecting was the cargo, and those new Colombian recruits. I doubt they planned on sending a welcoming committee. But what if they're expecting something else, as in weapons?"

"We received confirmation from the Panama Canal's customs officials. They boarded, checked papers and passports, and made a thorough inspection."

"No double hull?"

"No double hull. Look, we and the Israelis haven't had any proof she's transporting anything illegal, and even if we learn of something, once she's docked, I don't know if we -- or even the Colombian government -- will get any cooperation from port personnel. With the Quds in town, along with the guerrillas terrorizing, corruption is a way of life. And the Colombian authorities' involvement is still unclear, but we are investigating."

Grant's instincts started kicking in. "Sir, aside from the returning Colombians, what if the Quds *aren't* waiting for anyone or anything else to arrive? What if the *Al Sham* will provide transportation back to Syria for certain individuals, or maybe one individual in particular?"

"Shahbaz," Simmons quietly said. "Maybe that's a question for your G2, Captain. Think you can get an answer?"

"Unknown, sir, but we'll sure as hell try."

Simmons glanced at the clock on his desk. "Captain, I know you're short on time. I wish I had answers from Secretary McKinley and the Israelis, but I'm confident I'll hear something from him before you contact the LHD for your extraction. So, here's what I can do. I'll see that the ship is contacted and advised of your new set of orders. Then, you can confirm with the chopper crews when you're ready."

"Sounds good, sir. But should anything prevent us from making that initial contact, and we have to haul ass, do I have permission to . . .?"

"You do whatever you deem necessary to get yourselves and my men the hell outta there. The ship and chopper crews will remain on station."

"Yes, sir. Thank you."

"Just a second. As an FYI, the president has asked me to keep him informed of your progress, and wishes you well. That's it. Good luck."

Chapter 34

Grant looked toward the village, as he pressed the PTT. "Mike, any activity?"

"Not much. Vince was able to persuade most of them to stay indoors. They seemed to understand that the Iranians posted here were no longer a threat."

"Very well. Do all of you feel comfortable enough to report back here?"

The men reported simultaneously, "Affirm."

"Okay. C'mon back. I've got details from my talk with Simmons." Grant leaned over the railing. "Joe, bring the prisoners here. It'll be better for us to keep eyes on the property from this level."

"On our way."

Grant turned, seeing the three agents standing outside the doorway. "Gentlemen, hope you're all feeling better."

"We are," Salzman responded.

"Comin' up," Adler announced at the foot of the steps.

"Okay, Joe."

Slade, Milone, Stalley, and James stepped onto the deck, each hanging onto a prisoner, leading each into the house.

Novak and Kalinin hurried toward the northeast corner of the deck, prepared to stand watch.

With his arms crossed over his chest, Grant stared at the Iranians through narrowed eyes, as each man passed in front of him. Cammie shirts, unbuttoned and rumpled, hung outside their pants. Belts were missing. Boots were missing. Hair was disheveled. Once they were in the middle of the room, they were shoved onto their knees, then forced onto their stomachs. Ankles were immediately zip-tied.

Grant waved his four men toward him. With the upcoming discussion, and knowing the Iranians could understand English, Grant had to be extra cautious. He signaled to use earplugs on the UFs.

Adler kept his voice low. "I take it we've got some direction now?"

Grant nodded. "Any luck with the G2?"

"Not much. Those SOBs must've had their own form of SERE training (Survival, Evasion, Resistance, and Escape).

"That's freakin' disappointing," Grant commented, obviously irritated.

When his men finished their tasks, he motioned all of them, including the agents, away from the doorway, then said specifically to the agents, "Gentlemen, some of this will concern you. In the meantime, everyone needs to stand-by while I contact the LHD." Without revealing anything further, Grant walked to the far side of the house, then made his call.

Minutes later Grant reported to everyone that Condor 2 would arrive in under thirty minutes. Then he said, "Secretary McKinley spoke with the Israeli prime minister concerning our prisoners. I've notified the pilots that they'll be transporting the UFs to the ship." Grant looked toward the agents. "Condor 2 will also be providing your transportation, gentlemen. The appropriate personnel on the LHD are aware that you are to have use of their communication equipment."

"Understood. But what about you and your men?"

Salzman asked, surprised.

"Condor 1 is standing by, because we've got some other business to handle."

The agents knew not to question further, but Beatty asked, "Will we see you aboard ship?"

The right side of Grant's mouth curved up. "I certainly *hope* so! At least that's the plan for now. Oh, one more order from Langley. There will not be any communication with the prisoners. Once on-board the ship, they'll be stowed in the brig until a determination is made where their next, and probably final destination will be. Questions?"

Salzman asked, "Who's to be in charge of them while on the chopper?"

"I believe two masters at arms will be on-board. Anything else?"

"What about the dead, and their weapons?"

"Not your concern, sir." Grant left it at that, then moved on. "Okay. Vince, Nick, go to the village and prepare the civilians for the chopper's arrival, so they won't be scared shitless. Emphasize that they've all gotta be inside. C'mon back when you're sure they're secured." As the two hurried to their assignment, Novak took a position at the deck rail, raised his rifle, then adjusted the scope, keeping eyes on his two teammates running across the property.

"DJ." That was all Grant had to say. James nodded, then went to the southeast corner, with his sat phone in hand. Grant turned toward Slade and Stalley. "Ken, Doc, cut the restraints from the UFs' ankles. When Vince and Nick get back, the four of you take them to ground level. You've gotta be ready to lead them to the LZ as soon as that chopper touches dirt."

"Anything I can do?" Adler asked with a quick grin.

Grant laid a hand on Adler's shoulder, then said to the agents, "Gentlemen, sorry we didn't have time for official intros, but this is Joe Adler. Joe's been my partner in crime for many years." The agents introduced themselves, each offering a hand to Adler.

"Joe, let's give each room a thorough once-over before moving the gear down below, then we'll help Ken and Doc transfer the UFs."

Ten minutes later, Milone and Kalinin sprinted toward the house. Slowing their pace, they spotted Grant and Adler standing near the ground level door, hanging onto the UFs. Kalinin confirmed that all civilians were secured inside their homes.

"Okay, Nick. You and Vince hang onto these two." Glancing at his watch, Grant went toward the steps, and called up to James, "DJ, what's happening?"

James leaned over the railing showing Grant he was on the sat phone. He answered the call, "This is Tango 8."

Copilot Lieutenant Basquez spoke into his mic. "Tango 8, this is Condor 2. We are ten minutes from coordinates. Searchlight is on. We have two masters at arms on-board. Do you have instructions? Over."

"Will signal you with red light. Civilians are sheltered. Prisoners are secured. Be advised that your LZ is forty yards wide, East to West. That's all. Over."

"Roger. See you in a few, Tango 8. Condor 2, out."

"Boss," James called, as he was heading down the

steps. "Chopper will arrive in about nine minutes, with searchlight on. Two masters at arms are on-board."

"Okay, DJ." Grant removed his pen light from his vest, then pressed the PTT, specifically to update Novak. "Here's the order for boarding. First, the UFs. The masters at arms will take control. Next, Agents Salzman, Beatty, and Jacobs will take their gear. The Mossad agents' weapons and gear will be put on-board last."

Grant flipped down his NVGs, then sprinted down the property. Positioning himself on the east side, he looked west, and seeing the red searchlight, he turned on the pen light, then started waving the light high overhead.

Chapter 35

The four UFs continued struggling. Hearing the familiar sound of a chopper, their desperation increased. But their captors held them firmly, preventing them from escaping.

Jafari, in particular, wouldn't relinquish his continuing effort and tried wrenching his arm loose from Slade's grasp. But Slade had had enough, and with a fist, he walloped the back of Jafari's head, simultaneously releasing hold of his arm. Loosing control of his body, Jafari stumbled to the ground, his face smacking against compacted dirt. Slade immediately jerked him up, and squeezed his arm in a vice-like grip. A trickle of blood flowed from Jafari's left nostril. His face was speckled with dirt and other small particles of unknown origin. He lowered his head, conceding defeat.

Trees, brush whipped around. Leaves, flowers, dirt, grass were caught in a tornado-like environment. Condor 2 hovered briefly above its LZ, then began its descent. Once its wheels settled on the ground, Weinrich set the engines to idle. Spinning blades continued making the repetitive sound: *chuff, chuff, chuff, chuff.*

Grant ran to the open door on the left side, pointed to his men, then motioned them toward him. His four men clung tightly to the UFs' arms, practically dragging the captives toward the chopper.

Two masters at arms, each with a side holstered Beretta 92FS (designated the M9), stood at the edge of the open doorway. Petty Officer Lloyd shouted down at Grant, "Captain Stevens?!"

"That's me!" Grant replied, as he climbed aboard. He

shook each sailor's hand, then pointed toward the UFs. "Are you aware that the four prisoners are Iranians?"

"We are, sir."

"As an FYI, they speak fluent English. The agents coming aboard have been ordered not to converse with them."

"We received the order, sir, but not that they spoke English."

"Ready to come aboard!" Slade yelled, as he dropped four sets of boots, all strung together, just to the right of the doorway. He held onto Jafari, who still had blood dripping from his nose.

Grant backed away, as the guards assumed control. He leaned in toward the cockpit, and offered a hand. "Lieutenant Weinrich, Lieutenant Basquez, it's good to meet you, gentlemen."

"And you, sir," Weinrich responded.

Grant looked over his shoulder toward the cargo bay, seeing that the UFs were secured to tie downs on the deck. He turned again to the pilots. "It's gonna get crowded back there. The four agents are bringing their own gear, plus gear that belonged to a few other agents."

"We should be all right, sir. Oh, sir, Condor 1 is standing-by."

"Okay." Again Grant offered a hand. "Safe trip, gentlemen."

"Thanks, and good luck, sir," Weinrich said.

Grant jumped from the cargo bay, then smiled at the agents, as he reached for Salzman's offered hand. "Well, gentlemen, I promised you a ride."

Salzman clutched Grant's hand firmly. "We'll all

meet up in D.C. for a drink or two."

"Agent Nyland offered the same. It should be one helluva get together, sir."

"Well, maybe we can tack on steak dinners."

Grant tilted his head toward Adler. "Don't let Joe hear that." After noticing all gear was stowed, Grant said, "Listen, you'd better get aboard and get the hell outta here."

Basquez was leaning over his arm rest, looking toward the cargo bay. Seeing the three agents were aboard, he signaled Weinrich with a thumb's up.

Weinrich engaged the blades, opened the throttle completely, then slowly lifted the collective. The engines roared. Grant and his men backed away. As the chopper rose, the Team was buffeted by the downdraft.

As Condor 2's nose dipped, the men of A.T. each gave a quick, two-finger salute. Their actions were quickly reciprocated by three CIA agents, kneeling near the open doorway.

Grant turned his attention to Novak who was still on watch, and gave him a thumb's up. Only then did Novak relax.

The sound of the chopper hadn't yet faded, when Grant ordered, "Joe, give Vince the key to the truck. Vince, back it up close to the front steps." Milone started to leave when Grant said, "There are some civilians milling around. Make sure they know we're just borrowing it. And tell them to stay away from the house."

As Milone ran across the property, Grant noticed a faint light just below the eastern horizon. "C'mon, guys, we've got plenty of work to finish before we haul ass."

*

The Iranians' weapons and gear were piled behind the truck's cab. Then, in rapid succession, four bodies were dragged across the rough and splintered cargo bed, then laid near the weapons.

A.T.'s rucksacks had been put on-board. The men took defensive positions around the truck while Grant and Adler made another last minute inspection of both levels.

Adler backed out of the lower level, satisfied it was clear, then waited near the truck.

Grant grabbed both of the Iranians' walkie talkies, hurried out on deck, then snapped his fingers, getting Novak's attention. Both men hurried to ground level.

"Everybody," Grant gruffly called, then waited for his men to gather around him. Quickly, and in clear and concise instructions, Grant quietly laid out his plan. Then, "Questions?" Silence. "Okay" He handed James a walkie talkie. "DJ, in case the Quds start chatting."

"Vince, start the engine. Joe and I'll ride with you." Grant pointed toward the cargo bed. "Everybody else . . ." The men quickly took positions along the side rails. Stalley readied the camera. Novak was last in. Grant waited until they were settled, then climbed into the cab next to Adler. "Okay, Vince."

By now most lights were on in the village. People had gathered along the main street, talking among themselves, expressing their confusion from activities that happened over the past few hours. One thing they *were* sure of: the Iranians who had taken over their village, who made them work in the mine under extraordinary, painful, cruel conditions, had apparently been dealt with by another group of strangers.

They all went quiet, hearing the familiar puttering sound of their truck. Standing still, all they could do was watch as it drove past, the men inside paying little attention to them.

Chapter 36

Valle del Cauca
The Mine
Sunday
0610 Hours

The sun's rays were beginning to spread across the horizon. Even at such an early hour, the temperature was hovering close to eighty degrees.

Gripping his AK-47, Kasra Hashemi held the weapon by his side, as he paced in front of the mine's entrance. He was tired, hungry, and sweaty. He brushed sweat beads away from his forehead, while looking toward the base of the hill, picturing the cool, rushing water.

But beyond being uncomfortable, he was pissed. He and his fellow guard, Jalal Parsi, should have been relieved ten minutes ago. Never had the relieving guards been late, especially since they had responsibility for driving workers to the mine. And the work always started on schedule—except for this morning. But earlier they both heard what sounded like one, maybe two sounds similar to grenades, but neither smoke nor fire had been seen. The denseness of the jungle and the hills usually deadened normal sounds, even gunfire.

His brief respite from his angry thoughts was interrupted hearing Parsi announce, "There is still no sign of them."

Watching Parsi walk down the slope next to the entrance, Hashemi said, "There has been resistance by some of the workers in the past. Maybe one of us should walk to the village."

"No! Do you know what Imani would do?!" Parsi growled.

"Imani had no right to assume control over us!" Hashemi shot back. "*You* were in charge of all guards from the beginning!"

"Would you care to say that to his face, Kasra?!" Silence. "No! We must remain as long as it takes. Someone will show up."

Not bothering to further express his irritation, Hashemi pointed toward two large palms. "*You* can stand watch, then, while I take a break over there." He walked away, hooking his rifle strap on his shoulder.

Parsi shielded his eyes from a beam of sunlight that had broken through the trees. He backed up until he was at the mine entrance, then stood just outside the post and lintel framework, the heavy beams protecting the entrance from collapsing.

Seeing Hashemi in the shade, lying prone, with ankles crossed and eyes closed, Parsi looked at him with disdain. But he knew the moment of anger would pass. They were both frustrated with their assignment, guarding civilians, day after day, while many of their brethren had been given the opportunity to truly serve the cause. Even though the entire Quds Force stationed in Colombia was there for the same purpose, this position seemed belittling, meaningless, although, Shahbaz *had* designed the plan and functions of all teams. That fact was somewhat uplifting, but not entirely.

Leaning against a wooden beam, Parsi took out a red and white soft pack of Bahman cigarettes. Holding it in his palm suddenly brought back the days of the revolution of which he was a part. The brand was named for the eleventh month of the Iranian calendar, celebrating the revolution. He snapped a finger against the bottom of the pack, then removed a cigarette with his lips. Dropping the pack into his pocket, he lit a match, and held it near the tip of the cigarette.

His brain had no time to register the sound of a distant suppressed *clap,* when a heartbeat later a 7.62mm round penetrated his head just above the left temple, fragmenting bone, pulverizing brain matter. He dropped like a rock, never hearing the *crack* of the bullet.

Whichever sound had alerted him, Hashemi bolted upright, with his eyes settling on Parsi's crumbled body near the entrance. "Jalal!" Another *clap,* another 7.62, another *crack* with the same devastating results, the round striking Hashemi's forehead, making him unrecognizable.

Two hundred yards away, along the road traveled by the Ural trucks, the only other sound was Novak cycling the rifle bolt. He looked through the scope a moment longer before pushing himself up and onto his knees. He pressed the PTT. "Two UFs down."

"Copy that, Mike; meet you at the mine," Grant replied. Novak started fast jogging down the road.

Grant and Adler crabbed their way backwards from under an expanse of leaves and palm fronds, continuing to hold their high-power glasses. Finally in the open, they got up, and slid their MP5s around from their backs as they hurried to the truck. Adler was first in, then Grant, who ordered, "Move it, Vince!"

Chapter 37

CIA
Langley
Sunday
0720 Hours - Local Time

Sitting at a table in the cafeteria, with his white shirt sleeves rolled up and his tie loosened, Ray Simmons slid his coffee cup back and forth between his palms. He was looking toward the gardens beyond a bank of floor to ceiling, clear glass windows, but his mind was elsewhere.

He leaned back against the plastic chair, linking his fingers behind his head. Nothing was happening, no calls, no intercepts, no reports . . . and no demands. Neither the U-2 or satellite had detected any changes along the pipeline. *What the hell's going on?!* And there still hadn't been any further word from Stevens or the agents.

So deep in thought and worry, he failed to hear his deputy director call his name. Gordon was practically on top of him, when he called sharply, "Ray!"

Simmons snapped his head toward him. "What's wrong, Carl?!"

"Not what's wrong, Ray. Some good news. The agents are aboard the LHD. I've got Agent Salzman on hold on the scrambler."

"Hot damn! Let's go!"

Impatiently waiting as the elevator rose, Simmons asked, "Carl, how'd we get that call? I mean, it should've gone to the DDO, Harry Franklin."

"It did, but he had it transferred. He should be waiting outside your office."

Rushing along the hallway, the two men spotted Franklin standing near the closed door. Simmons offered a hand to the DDO. "Harry, thanks for transferring the call. C'mon in."

*

Simmons pressed the switch on the conference phone, as he, Gordon and Franklin were rolling out chairs from under the conference table. "Agent Salzman, Ray Simmons here. I understand you're all safely aboard the LHD."

"We are, Mr. Director. Sir, Agents Beatty and Jacobs are here with me. We're scheduled to go to sickbay for an eval once we're done here, but I can tell you that for the most part, we're okay."

"Good. Good. Glad to hear it. Before we start, Deputy Director Franklin is joining me, along with my Deputy Director Carl Gordon. Listen, we all send our condolences for Agent Kaufman. Losing a team member is always difficult."

"We appreciate that, Mr. Director. But at least we know he's going home with us, sir, thanks to Grant Stevens and his men."

"Yes, he informed me." A quiet moment passed, before Simmons began, "Agents Nyland and Sands filled me in with as much as they knew. The last I talked with Captain Stevens, he gave me all of the details, mostly in bullet form, but more than enough."

"Uh, sir, did you say *Captain* Stevens? No one ever

mentioned ranks."

"No surprise there. He and his men were SEALs. I don't know if you've ever heard of Team Alpha Tango, but . . ."

"Oh, hell, yes! And that was them?! Damn!"

The three men quietly chuckled, then Simmons said, "Gentlemen, we've got all the time you need. So, why don't you start from the beginning, from when you reached the meeting location?"

For a solid ninety minutes, the three agents gave their report and answered questions, knowing they'd go through a full debrief once they were back in D.C.

*

Satisfied they'd received enough information on the agents' mission to pass along to the president, and all other pertinent departments and individuals, Simmons asked, "Did Captain Stevens discuss what he had planned once you departed?"

"Not really. They were all pretty closed mouth about that."

"Not surprising," Simmons said with a quick smile.

Gordon rolled his chair back, and went to answer a knock at the door. He scanned the sheet of paper as he walked back to the table. "Oh shit," he said under his breath, then handed the paper to Simmons.

"Agent Salzman, I'm putting you on hold." Simmons didn't wait for any response, but immediately read the intel report. "Holy . . .!"

"What?!" Franklin asked, obviously concerned.

"The Quds. They gave a sample of their intentions should upcoming demands not be met."

He handed the paper to Franklin who read: an operations building near Magdalena was hit by an RPG. Three operators on duty were killed. Four pump stations were temporarily shut down. A CIA listening post picked up a transmission from an unsecured sat phone to the office of Miguel Montoya. The message was very brief, but it confirmed the attack.

"Montoya again," Franklin said, snapping a finger against the paper. "He's been walking a fine line lately, considering Colombia knows he's interacted with a number of guerrilla organizations and drug dealers."

"True," Simmons said, "but they're also aware that he and his family have been threatened by the right-wing guerrilla group, the PCA (Populist Colombian Army)."

Franklin asked, "So, you think he's being used by the government, and without his knowledge? I mean, he is the assistant minister of their security service."

"There's one way to find out, Harry. We can use that intercept report and contact the minister. He can handle it from there." Simmons finally noticed the blinking light on the phone. "Agent Salzman, sorry you had to wait. Look, you three need to get to sickbay. I'm sure Director Franklin will keep me advised when you're due home. Safe trip, gentlemen."

"Thank you, Mr. Director," all three agents responded.

As the call ended, Simmons immediately asked Gordon, "What about sat images? Anything?"

"Nothing yet."

When the intercom buzzed, Simmons knew it was his secretary. "Yes, Gloria?"

"Secretary McKinley's on line two."

"Thanks, Gloria." As he was ready to press the button, he said quietly to Gordon, "Sure as hell hope there's been a breakthrough with any demands." He answered the call. "Mr. Secretary?"

"Ray, you've read the intel report concerning the Quds' attack?"

"We have. Sir, as an FYI, Deputy Director Franklin and Deputy Director Gordon are here."

McKinley acknowledged the two men, "Gentlemen." Then he began, "That report was issued just prior to our receiving a specific demand from the Quds concerning the hostages. And before you ask, they still don't know about the agents being rescued. I've already updated the president, but when the Iranians will be informed of the rescue is still an open question."

"I have to assume, and hope," Simmons said, "that it won't be until Captain Stevens and his men are safely out of the country."

"We can only give our opinions and suggestions, Ray. The final say so won't rest with us. Okay, getting back to the demand. They want to exchange the three hostages for Ashem Lajani, who's been held in our maximum security prison for nearly three years. I'm sure that name's familiar, Ray."

"He was captured six months after the bombing of our embassy in Mali."

"Look, I just wanted to update you, and inform you there'll be a Sit Room meeting at two o'clock. Maybe we'll all have additional intel by then. Do you have any-thing else to add?"

"We just spoke to Agent Salzman. He and Agents Beatty and Jacobs gave us a brief report before they were to report to sickbay. But he assured us they were doing okay."

"I'm very pleased to hear that. You'll have a chance to fill us in further during the meeting. Anything else?"

Simmons glanced at Franklin, who shook his head. "No, sir."

"All right. I'll see you at the White House." End of call.

The men rolled their chairs back, as Simmons said, "Harry, can you get me a detailed report by noon?"

Franklin glanced at his watch. "No problem." He immediately left.

Simmons stacked the papers. "C'mon, Carl. Let's organize the notes we took from Stevens' report."

Chapter 38

Valle del Cauca
The Mine
0620 Hours - Local Time

"There's Mike," Adler said, pointing toward the windshield. Novak was near the entrance, standing over a body.

"Vince," Grant said, "back it up."

Milone made a U-turn, then slowly backed up toward the entrance, leaving enough room for the Team to maneuver gear and bodies. Everyone was out of the cab and cargo bed before the engine stopped sputtering.

Grant mustered alongside Novak. "Mike?"

"Yeah, boss."

Grant looked down at the body, and at what used to be a head. He laid a hand on Novak's shoulder. "You okay?"

"Sure, boss."

Grant tugged on Novak's sleeve. "C'mon, we've got work to do." *Maybe he and I need to have a talk later,* Grant thought.

Standing behind the truck, Grant began laying out the plan. "Joe, Doc, you'll come with me to inspect inside. Doc, take pictures. DJ, Vince, you've got first watch. Nick, Ken, start unloading the UFs' weapons. Mike, keep the timers in their container, then put it and the explosives in one bag. Okay, guys, turn to."

Adler and Stalley followed Grant into the mine, having no idea what they'd find, but they immediately noticed unpleasant odors. About ten yards in from the entrance, another tunnel bore off to the left. Grant took out his pen light, and took a few steps toward it. Its mere five foot width and height disturbed him. *How the hell did they work in here?* He aimed the beam toward the rear. "Can't be more than thirty feet long," he commented before moving the beam side to side, the light settling on canvas sacks, shovels and pickaxes leaning against the rocky sides. "C'mon. Let's try the main tunnel."

The light shining in from the entrance slowly faded the farther in they walked. Flipping down their NVGs, they scanned the rocky side walls and overhead of the eight-foot wide by barely seven-foot high space, obviously carved out with manual tools. The ground consisted of loose, but mostly compacted dirt, along with crushed rocks. Rough hewn logs, forming post and lintels, had been spaced every ten feet.

They'd passed under four supports, and with their eyes now adjusted to the dark, they flipped up the NVGs, and turned on their pen lights, shining them along the walls.

"What the . . .?" Grant said, as the pen light beam settled on a dozen canvas sacks piled against a wall.

"Are those what I think they are?" Adler asked as they knelt near the sacks.

Grant untied one. Veins of gold within the rocks glittered in the pen light's beam. "All the villagers' work and sweat, ready to be shipped to Iran."

Adler briefly glimpsed into the bag before retying it, then lifting it. "Must weigh about fifteen pounds. Guess the weight had to be kept low because of the kids. Do we leave them here, or distribute to the villagers?"

"Gotta think about it. Let's keep goin'."

They'd walked another thirty feet when suddenly they came to a standstill. "Bingo!" Adler's voice echoed.

Lined up along both sides, with a pathway down the center, were wooden crates, each labeled as containing Russian-made SAMs; warheads; RPG launchers; RPG grenades; grenades; ammo boxes; boxes with AK-47s and Browning pistols.

"Doc, pictures—right now. Take closeups that'll show labels."

"Jesus," Adler said under his breath. "There might be enough here to destroy the whole damn mountain."

"Don't think that's what they had in mind, but, yeah, it sure as hell could. Now it means our plans have changed."

"As in, we can't let any of it detonate?"

"Right, Joe." Grant blew out a long breath, then pressed the PTT. "Mike, bring in the bag with the equipment. We're in the right side tunnel about a thirty-five yards in."

"On my way."

Echoes of hurried footsteps alerted Grant that Novak was closing in. "Here ya go, boss," Novak said, carefully laying down the bag.

"Thanks, Mike. All quiet out front?"

"So far. What else can I do?"

Grant called over his shoulder, "Doc, how ya doing?"

"A couple more should do it."

"When you're done, you and Mike go check the tunnel next door. Take pictures, but be careful. It's claustrophobic in there." Within a few minutes Stalley and Novak were headed back to the entrance and then side tunnel. Grant pressed the PTT and whispered, "Ken, Nick, once Mike's in that left tunnel, drag in those two fresh bodies. Follow the right side tunnel thirty yards in. Posthaste, guys, posthaste."

"Roger," Slade responded.

"Outta sight, outta mind?" Adler questioned knowing Grant was taking the action because of Novak.

"Maybe just outta sight, Joe."

"Is he okay?" Adler asked with concern in his voice.

Grant shrugged his shoulders. "Thinking of having a talk when I get a chance."

Hearing the hurried shuffling of feet, then seeing Slade and Kalinin each holding onto an arm of a UF, Grant pointed, "Drag them all the way to the back, then get me a rough estimate on that distance and number of support beams."

Shortly after, Slade and Kalinin jogged back to Grant. Slade reported, "From here to the end is about forty feet."

"Four support structures," Kalinin said.

"Okay, guys."

The two started to leave, when Kalinin asked, "You want us to bring in the other bodies?"

"Not just yet, Nick, but bring their weapons. Get everything outta the cargo bed, ready to drive the truck back to the village."

Adler pointed to the ground, then moved his arm, as if following an invisible line leading to the entrance. "The UFs left themselves plenty of extra space to bring in more 'boomers.'"

Grant nodded, just as Novak and Stalley returned. Stalley's face, hands, and cammies were covered in dirt and dust. "I crawled to the back, boss. There were some buckets, a couple sets of bellows, and what looked like sections of a wooden trough. All the tools and sacks were up front. I guess you saw those."

"Okay. Listen, take all our canteens to the river. It should be safe to drink if you go upstream a little extra."

"I'll drop in iodine tablets in case there are any nasties, boss," Stalley commented.

As Stalley turned away, Grant grabbed his arm. "Doc, thanks for crawling that 'extra mile.'"

"Sure, boss."

Once they'd gone, Grant turned his attention to the position of each support, then started making mental calculations. "It'll work," he mumbled. He picked up the bag, then called, "C'mon, Joe."

"Where ya goin'?"

Grant pointed. "To that beam." He got on a knee, then removed one block at a time from the bag. Each military grade C-4 (M112) block measured 2"x1.5"x11" and resembled modeling clay. He stripped off the Mylar film, then using his K-bar, sliced each block into small sections, laid them side-by-side, then started on the next block.

Adler looked back toward the weapons, then knelt next to him. "Now I know where you're going with this."

Grant grinned. "It should work, shouldn't it, Joe?"

"Damn straight it will," Adler said, drawing out his K-bar.

Chapter 39

Once the blocks had been cut then organized near the timers, Grant picked up a few of each. "Okay, Joe. I'll start here, you there."

The two men worked in tandem, moulding the C-4 around a joint, pressing in a timer, then inserting a red and a blue wire into the explosive.

As he moved under the middle section of the beam, Grant asked Adler, "Think we should put a very small amount on the beams above the weapons?"

"We can do that if all you want is to weaken 'em."

"That's all."

"Consider it done. Hey, does this remind you of another cave, another time?"

Grant secured a timer in the C-4, then started inserting the two wires. "Yeah, Sicily, but at least this time there isn't a freakin' exploding volcano."

"But it sure was satisfying watching that big, beautiful yacht go *BOOM*!"

*

They finished the process together. From where they began to where the weapons starting lining up was more than a safe distance. Adler cut a block of C-4 in half. "That should do it. I'll chop it up as I go. Be right back." Taking the block and timers, he started a quick jog, going deeper into the tunnel.

"I'll be at the entrance," Grant called over his shoulder, walking away with the bag. As he reached the entrance, Stalley and Novak were handing out the canteens.

"Everybody, suck up enough water," Grant said. "It's just gonna get hotter in a couple of hours." He pointed to Milone, James, Slade, and Kalinin, saying, "When you're done, bring the last bodies to the main tunnel. Stow them at the far back. Joe should be done with the final installs by the time you get there."

Stalley handed Grant's canteen to him, and as the four men started dragging four bodies past him, Grant stopped them. "Hold up. Listen, I know this will mean extra time and work, and I know you're hot and tired, but there are a dozen canvas sacks. I wanna take them to the villagers. It was their hard work that filled them. Mike, stand watch. Everybody else follow me."

While the bodies were being dragged to the rear of the tunnel, Grant carried two sacks to the truck, then ran back inside the mine.

Once the task had been completed, they drank from their canteens, finishing the last mouthfuls. Stalley pointed with a thumb over his shoulder. "There's plenty more where that came from."

Grant poured the cool water into his hand, then wiped it over his face. "Okay, Doc. Do you have enough energy left to . . ."

"Absolutely, boss," Stalley said, quickly gathering the canteens.

"I'll go with you," Milone said, seeing Grant give him the okay.

Grant first pointed toward the small tunnel. "Joe, there aren't any supports in there." He then pointed overhead. "Think this beam would be enough to do the job?"

221

Adler wiped sweat from his face, while calculating the distance. "It should, but maybe put a small section of a block just inside the tunnel, if you wanna be sure "

"You take care of that, while I start on this beam."

Within minutes, all C-4 and timers had been secured. As Grant and Adler walked toward the truck, they heard Slade, "Here come Doc and Vince."

Grant looked overhead, squinting in the bright sunlight. "Maybe we can stash the NVGs, guys. Sunglasses will be a helluva lot better."

Once the canteens had been distributed, and the men drank their fill, and rubbed some on their faces and necks, Grant got down to business. "Vince, drive back the way we came, and go at least a quarter mile." Grant swiped his arm sideways toward the cargo bed, ordering, "Everybody in!"

"What the fuck! You gotta be shittin' me, boss!" Slade roared.

"Ken, get the hell in the truck! *Everybody* in the truck! Do it, dammit!"

"You heard him!" Adler shouted.

Grant swung around, just as Adler stepped closer, holding a remote. Looking up at Grant through ice blue eyes, Adler snarled, "Don't even think it."

Grant smiled and slapped his shoulder, then started to order Milone to move out, when Novak got Grant's attention and appealed, "Boss, please. You've gotta let me stay. Somebody's gotta keep eyes on," he said, pointing toward the road heading north.

"Let him," Adler whispered out of the corner of his

mouth.

Grant knew it was the right decision, and for more than one reason. "C'mon, Mike." Novak jumped from the truck, then ran parallel to the road, heading close to his previous position, but this time selecting a place with much better protection from the ensuing explosion.

Grant signaled Milone. "Go!"

Milone shifted into gear, then stepped on the gas. Grant and Adler waited until the truck was nearly out of sight, then they raced down the same road for nearly a hundred yards. "There!" Grant shouted. They swerved off the road, then holding down their helmets, they jumped into a ditch, immediately getting on their knees.

Grant pressed the PTT. "Mike, you ready?!"

"Affirm!"

"Vince, where you at?"

"Stopped about one quarter mile! Ready!"

Grant and Adler inserted their earplugs, then, on their bellies, crabbed their way backwards until they were barely able to see over the edge of the ditch.

"Ready," Adler said, holding the remote.

Grant nodded, and pressed the PTT, allowing his men to hear the countdown. "On one." Adler flipped up the orange safety cover. Grant began, "Three . two . one!" Grant immediately released the PTT button, as Adler pressed the remote's firing button. Both of them instantly lowered their heads.

A mere second after the violent blast, a shockwave tore through the area. A huge orange-red-yellow fireball billowed high above the hill. The earth above the tunnels blew apart, with chunks of rocks, splintered wood beams, dirt, shooting out in every direction. Large rocks, some fragmented, blasted upward as if shot out of a cannon, then immediately began falling, pummeling the ground inside and around the hole, creating continuous deep-sounding *thuds*.

Grant, Adler, and Novak covered the back of their necks with one hand, while pulling the front edges of their T-shirts over their mouths and noses, as an immense cloud of dust began descending on them. Shards of wood, stones, dirt, clumps of grass rained down, struck their backs, *pinged* against their helmets.

Keeping his head lowered, Grant pulled out an earplug, then inserted his earpiece, as he heard Kalinin calling, "Grant, Joe, Mike, come in!"

"Nick, wait one! Joe, you okay?!"

"Yeah. Okay. Damn! That was loud!"

"Mike?!"

"I'm okay."

"Mike, head to us. We've gotta haul ass ASAP!"

"Roger!" Novak sprung to his feet, then sprinted down the road.

Grant continued holding down the PTT. "Vince, pick us up!"

"On our way!"

Climbing out of the ditch, Grant and Adler hastily dusted themselves off, as they fixed their eyes on the rubble. "Looks like it worked, Joe," Grant laughed.

"Was there any doubt in our military minds that it wouldn't?" Staying focused on the destruction, Adler commented, "I don't expect there'll be any delayed explosions from the Iranian shit inside."

Grant looked over Adler's shoulder. "Here comes Mike, and I hear the truck. Joe, did Ken give you the key for the agents' Nissan?"

Adler patted his vest, when a sudden thought crossed his mind. "Wait. Are you . . .? You aren't thinking about . . ."

"Taking a trip to the docks?"

"Yeah. That's it."

"First, we've gotta try and explain to the villagers what happened, then time will tell." Grant focused on Novak. "You okay?"

"Affirmative, boss; enjoyed the fireworks."

Grant placed a reassuring hand on Novak's shoulder, giving him a quick smile.

The truck skidded to a stop as Milone hit the brakes. Grant and Adler ran to the cab. In the rear, Slade and Kalinin reached down, latched onto Novak's arms, and hauled him into the cargo bed. They started roughly slapping at Novak's cammies. "You're a mess!" Slade laughed, as dust and other particles fell from Novak.

Milone shifted into first, as Grant said, "Vince, head to the village, then drive to the shed so we can offload the bags. Go!" In the cargo bed, the men grabbed onto the sides as the truck suddenly picked up speed.

As they headed toward the village, Grant had a moment of remorse. *Did I just totally screw up those people's lives by taking away their ability to mine for gold? How were they going to react?* Turning over the canvas sacks might satisfy them, until he told them the sacks had to be buried, at least temporarily.

But his concern extended beyond that. Once he and

his men departed would the entire town become a target for the Quds, and especially from Shahbaz once the destruction had been discovered? Hiding the weapons in the mine had to have been ordered by the Iranian, and probably approved by Tehran. *But why that mine? Or maybe it wasn't the only one. Had the Quds made any attacks along the pipeline?* "More questions," Grant grumbled, before changing his thought direction.

He had to call in the chopper to extract them, and then contact Langley. Would Simmons approve his idea for boarding the *Al Sham* while it was anchored in the channel, or maybe take more drastic measures once it had begun its return to Syria? Would his request go all the way to the top, to the president?

"Hey!" Adler said, poking his elbow against Grant.
"What?"

"Sorry to snap you out of your daydreaming, but we have arrived."

Chapter 40

Aquilla

The villagers had gathered in the field. All eyes continued looking in the direction of billowing smoke, the direction of a blast that shook them emotionally. Voices seemed to merge as they openly wondered and worried where all this chaos would lead. This day had been like no other. Hearing an engine, then seeing their truck, they were grateful the strangers were returning it as promised.

Milone made a sharp turn behind the buildings, continued driving across the rutted ground, then backed up close to the shed. The Team offloaded the canvas sacks, put them in two rows, then covered them with grain sacks.

Milone drove everyone back to the corner building, then parked the truck as they had found it, with the cab facing the road.

Once they had met at the back of the truck, Grant asked Kalinin, "Have you seen any kids?"

"Yeah, several," Kalinin answered.

"Joe, let me have some Snickers." Grant put the candy in his vest, then said, "Vince, I'll go with you. Everybody else, go with Joe to the Nissan." Adler led the five men toward the rear of the east side buildings.

As Grant and Milone rounded the corner, and seeing several village men walking toward them, they slid their MP5s around to their backs, then took off their helmets, trying anything to appear less threatening. They had enough to answer for.

Questions came at them fast and furious. Milone first tried to calm them, then translated and responded as best he could, especially about the canvas sacks, and the need to bury them quickly.

While Milone was talking, Grant noticed a few children, hanging close to the adults. He took out the candy bars, knelt on a knee, then held the candy in his open palm. Looking up at one of the adult women, he smiled, then lifted his hand, as if offering her the candy. She led three of the children closer, speaking softly to them. Timidly, each child walked to Grant, snatched a candy bar, then ran back to her. She smiled at Grant, then walked away with the children.

Suddenly, Grant and Milone heard Adler in their ear-pieces. "Ken has eyes on vehicle, three hundred yards, coming from the East! Move it!"

"Roger!" Grant swiveled his MP5 around from his back as he shouted to Milone, "Get them inside! Now!"

Moving quickly toward the villagers, Milone motioned them to run. Then he pointed toward the buildings, again yelling the order. The villagers scattered when they finally understood. Adults scooped up children in their arms then dashed into the nearest building.

Grant remained near the end building, ready with his MP5, as he kept an eye on Milone, who was running to the far end of the village, ensuring all residents were off the street. Grant pressed the PTT, "C'mon, Vince!"

Milone raced behind Grant, then the two took off around the corner, running like hell behind the buildings where the agents' Nissan was parked, still covered with netting.

Adler poked his head out from around the front of the Nissan, and called gruffly, "C'mon! C'mon!" before he headed for the trees.

Grant and Milone skidded around the Nissan nearly losing their footing, then immediately caught up to Adler. As they got to the edge of the tree line, they dove for the dirt, then immediately crabbed their way deeper into the jungle. Most of the men were already on their bellies, ready with their weapons.

Adler whispered to Grant, "Ken," while he pointed South toward Slade's position, nearer to the road, but still hidden. Adler then pointed North. "Mike." Novak had positioned himself near the shed where he had a good view of the target house.

Slade whispered into his throat mic, "One hundred yards and closing."

Chapter 41

Slade remained perfectly still, except for his thumb pressing down the PTT. "Vehicle is another Nissan SUV, black, windows open," he whispered into his throat mic.

"Copy that," Grant responded quietly.

The vehicle slowed as it was passing the agents' vehicle, which gave Slade a slightly clearer view of its occupants. As it was driving away, he reported, "Eyes on three, no, five UFs, two front, three rear."

The vehicle continued on, slowed again opposite where the farm truck was parked, then continued toward the house. Once it was far enough from his position, Slade crabbed his way forward moving closer to a large leafy bush. Sliding his shotgun around to his back, then getting on his belly, he pressed the PTT. "Vehicle at end of road, turning toward house." A second later he reported, "No longer have eyes on."

"Maintain position, Ken," Grant whispered, then focused on Novak, who was the only one with a clear view of the house. "Mike, you have eyes on yet?"

"Affirm. Vehicle stopped about fifteen yards from house."

"Copy." Grant's concerns mounted. *Did the UFs hear the explosion? Did they investigate? If not, had they tried contacting the men at the mine using a radio or sat phone? That could be why they're here. No one answered.*

If that were the case, and now not seeing any of their counterparts, undoubtedly increased their suspicions. Those suspicions would prove to be fact once they discovered the hostages were gone. Finding bloodstains inside and out would ignite those suspicions, turning them to anger. He expected their focus to immediately center on the village residents.

They've gotta be stopped, Grant thought, *and before they start back toward the village; have to prevent collateral damage.* To add to the problem, whatever was to happen, would happen in broad daylight. A tentative plan sped through Grant's brain. He relayed instructions to his men.

*

The driver, and front and left rear UFs exited the vehicle. Turan Rahbar had hurried around to the left rear passenger door, and opened it. Major Tannaz Asadi exited, followed by Izad Mohsen. Remaining next to the vehicle, Asadi perused the front property, then looked toward the house, that seemed as quiet as a tomb.

Asadi ordered, "You will throughly search and investigate inside and out. Izad and I will remain here." Rahbar nodded then signaled the other two men. Mohsen went to the rear of the vehicle, holstered his pistol, raised the tailgate, then removed an AK-47. He hooked the strap on his shoulder, placed his hand outside the weapon's trigger guard, then returned to Asadi.

*

Grant waited impatiently. "Mike, update."
"Three with pistols in hand."
"Any rifles?"

"One AK. Wait one. We have movement. One UF walking property, south side; second inspecting outside lower level; third one on second level walking toward back deck; two outside vehicle, west side; one has the AK."

"We're moving toward road; will wait for your signal to cross to south side. Ken and DJ will be first across, then Ken will handle signaling us. Ken, you copy?"

"Copy."

Grant continued holding down the PTT. "Vince, Doc, position yourselves in or near the first and last buildings. You've gotta ensure all those villagers remain off the street."

Milone and Stalley bolted from the trees, making their way around the agents' Nissan. Milone ran to the corner building closer to the road; Stalley, the opposite end of the village. Slowly edging their way toward the front, they quietly reported, "In position."

Novak reported, "Two UFs now around back, third is entering first floor doorway. Get ready." Novak's voice changed to a louder whisper: "Go! Go!"

Slade and James took off, not stopping until they were close to the trees, then hit the dirt, crawling for more cover.

Slade reported he and James were in position. With eyes on the house, Slade signaled Kalinin, then Grant and Adler.

Grant notified Novak that they were all on the south side, were moving in the direction of the house, then would take positions opposite the field. That was the best Grant could do to prevent any crossfire or rounds being fired into the village.

With his men now having eyes on the house and the UFs by the vehicle, Grant had to reassign Novak. "Mike, move to our last position. You, Vince, and Nick, will be last defense if UFs make it past us. Everybody copy?"

Three quiet responses came back: "Copy."

Novak then reported, "On my way."

Holding down the PTT, Grant whispered, "Ken, near Joe." Slade crabbed backwards, then changing direction, he headed toward Adler, coming up from behind him. He quietly positioned next to Adler.

Team A.T. was ready. They waited.

Chapter 42

Farzad Jahandar began scouring the property at the rear of the house, while Piruz Zare walked the front area before inspecting inside.

On the upper deck at the back of the house, Turan Rahbar walked slowly, pausing briefly to look in each of the partially open windows. Both rooms were dark, and appeared to be empty. He turned the corner and headed to the front of the house, when his eyes were drawn to dark stains on the deck. He knelt down and touched one. It was dry but it was definitely blood.

Zare stepped inside the lower level. Clutching his pistol with both hands, he inspected the main room, then each of the bedrooms. As he started backing out of the main room, he heard Rahbar call, "Piruz! Farzad!"

Zare ran up the front steps, Jahandar the rear, both hurrying toward Rahbar. For a moment, the three were quiet, staring down at the bloody streaks.

Rahbar's eyes went to each man as he asked, "Did either of you find anything suspicious?"

Both men shook their heads, with Zare responding, "Nothing in three rooms. It were as if no one had been inside."

One behind the other the three took hurried steps toward the closed front door. Rahbar leaned over the railing, calling to Asadi, "Stay there!" Stopping in front of the door, he caught sight of another red trail leading underneath it. His questions mounted, his anger increased, and with all his force, he kicked the door open.

They cautiously entered, immediately noticing a bloodstain. But their eyes soon trained on a wide, smeared trail leading toward a bedroom.

Rahbar's stomach tightened. His fingers curled around the pistol grip, as he and the two men followed the trail into the room, where it ended at another irregular-shaped stain.

So much blood. Whoever this was, surely died almost instantly, Rahbar thought.

Even without searching the other bedroom, he knew they would not find anyone, not the hostages, not the guards from the mine, and not Imani and his men. But he sent Zare to the bedroom anyway.

Within a moment Zare returned. "Nothing; there was nothing in there."

"Not even blood?"

"Nothing!"

Rahbar started turning a slow three sixty, with his eyes focusing on the ceiling and each wall, checking every surface. *How did this happen?! There are no bullet holes; no damage, no evidence whatsoever.*

Confused, he walked slowly onto the deck, with the two men following him. Focusing on the village, he wondered, *Is it possible?! Those villagers would certainly have knives, and more likely, machetes, which would account for the heavy blood loss, and lack of bullet holes.*

Jahandar and Zare went around him, walked down to the first level, then waited. Rahbar stood at the top of the stairs, fixing his eyes on them. *They saw the blood. They know there was no damage, no evidence of shots having been fired. But will they support me with my idea?*

The farm truck caught his attention. *How convenient*

for transporting bodies. The presence of blood stains in the cargo bed might prove his theory. But an interrogation of the villagers, or just the threat of, might confirm what he suspected. *Major General Khorasani, and Tehran will demand answers.*

*

Twenty-five yards from the house, at a thirty degree angle, five men maintained their positions, hidden far enough off the road in the midst of and under varying height palms, ferns, and thick greenery, but each man had a clear view of the road. They ignored, but were very aware of possible crawling, poisonous creatures. Yet, they stayed focused, heart rates remained normal.

Lying on their bellies near one another, Grant and Adler were using their high-power glasses. None of the three UFs that had inspected the property looked familiar. The face of the UF who'd retrieved the AK was visible only briefly. The fact that what or how many weapons were inside the vehicle was troubling.

Grant moved his glasses slightly, trying to see the UF standing by the vehicle's left side passenger door. All he saw was the top portion of a green ball cap.

He silently wondered, *Why are all of them wearing field combat uniforms and ball caps, and not cammies like the other group?* He had zeroed in on uniform patches as the three men came from the house. *A second and a first lieutenant, and . . . a captain.* He lowered the glasses, while silently questioning, *No enlisted? Not likely they're the two waiting by the vehicle. Who the hell are they?!*

Whoever they were they had to be more involved with the Quds' plan. He was sure of it—and he wanted answers. He pressed the PTT, whispering, "I want at least one of those bastards alive. Nick, DJ, ready Sigs." Kalinin and James carefully swiveled the MP5s around to their backs, drew their pistols, then heard Grant continue, "Prepare for flash-bang. Word is 'echo.'"

*

Zare called from the ground level, "Turan, it is time we update . . ."

"Yes. Yes." Rahbar joined the two men, then led them toward the waiting Asadi.

"What happened? Did you find anyone?" Asadi asked anxiously. Each man reported what he had seen, confirming one another's story.

Then, looking directly at Asadi, Rahbar said, "I would like to tell you my theory."

Asadi stepped closer, with eyes narrowed. "I do not want to hear a theory that it was *our* men who did this. Do I make myself clear?!"

"Of course, Major. Of course."

When Rahbar finally finished, Asadi asked with skepticism, "Are you intending for me to believe that not one shred of evidence, aside from blood, was found in that house?"

"I am."

Asadi waited a moment while continuing in thought, finally asking, "Have you even considered that the hostages could have freed themselves, and had overtaken our men?"

"Three hostages, overtaking at least five, if not eight trained, armed men?"

"Why not?! Those Americans were well trained in the art of combat. We know that many of those with the CIA were selected from their special operations forces, who all went through SERE training. So, I ask you again, Turan. Why not?!"

Rahbar let the idea roll around in his mind, before answering, "It is very possible, but I still believe the villagers were responsible, or at least somehow involved." He pointed toward the village. "Our mens' vehicle, and the Americans' vehicle are still down there. Why did the Americans not make their escape in their own vehicle?" Asadi remained silent. Rahbar reiterated, "We *must* inspect that truck. If there are blood stains or any other evidence, we will know."

"No matter what we learn here," Asadi said, "we still must inspect the mine, and check the inventory." *The mine!* Asadi suddenly thought. *Was the distant sound we heard an explosion?! Could it have been at the mine? What if Rahbar is correct? What if the villagers transported the bodies to the mine? There were more than enough weapons to cause such an explosion!*

Rahbar interrupted Asadi's thoughts. "Major Asadi?"

Pointing toward the village, Asadi said, "We have not seen anyone since we arrived. Jahandar, first drive near that truck, then along the main street. We will watch for any signs of movement or sounds from inside those buildings. If no one appears, the three of you will go building to building, searching for anyone to interrogate, even if that person is a child. Perhaps one of you should make a quick search inside the tree line. Someone has to be in that village. They did not just disappear. Once your search has begun, Izad will drive me to the mine. Have I made myself clear?"

"Yes. We understand," Rahbar answered.

Vehicle doors slammed shut. Jahandar started the engine.

*

Grant and Adler quickly stashed their glasses. Adler had his Sig in hand, as Grant laid his on the ground in front of him, then removed a flash-bang from his vest. His men aimed their weapons.

Farther down the road, Novak went through the same process with his sniper rifle. Milone and Kalinin kept eyes on the deserted main street, watching for anyone who might try to step outside. The residents had heeded their warnings, but if they happened to be near a window when the flash-bang exploded, they should only feel some residual effects.

In under a minute Team A.T. would confront another group of UFs, and perhaps the most significant ones.

Chapter 43

1045 Hours

Jahandar backed the Nissan close to the road, shifted into gear, then made a wide turn. Feeling the tires meet compacted dirt, he guided the vehicle slowly downhill.

The Iranians kept eyes on the village, with fully loaded pistols in hand, except for Jahandar, who had his pistol in his lap, and Mohsen, who had the butt of his AK-47 resting on his thigh, the barrel pointing up. Aside from engine noise, and tires crunching over small stones, there was nothing but silence in the vehicle.

Little did the Iranians know—that was all about to change.

Grant crabbed his way closer to a location where he wouldn't have any obstructions when he threw the grenade. Hugging the ground, he raised his head just enough to see the approaching vehicle and a front seat passenger. Hoping his timing was perfect, he pressed the PTT and whispered, "Echo!" Quickly getting on a knee, he hurled the grenade, then lowered his head, closed his eyes, and plugged his ears.

The grenade landed with a *clang* on the Nissan's hood, exploding into a sudden brilliant white flash, accompanied by an ear-splitting sound, leaving the UFs temporarily blinded, groaning from a constant, painful ringing in their ears. Jahandar lost all sight of the road. With both hands pressed against his ears, the car started drifting toward the trees, and toward A.T.

Grant was shouting, "Go! Go! Go!" The men sprang to their feet, racing from their hiding places. Slade, who was out in front, aimed the shotgun, then fired off one round at the engine, pumped the weapon, then fired another at the front tire, causing the vehicle to veer even further toward the trees. Its forward momentum was finally blocked by two large palms.

The men went into a shooter's stance: Grant was just forward of and a few yards away from the front passenger door; Adler, the same near the driver's door; James, just aft and to the side of the right rear door; Kalinin, the same at the left rear door; Slade was near the tailgate, pointing the shotgun at the rear window.

Keeping his eyes on the Iranians, Grant quietly said to James, "Now, DJ."

James immediately shouted in Farsi, "Drop your weapons! Hands on your heads! Exit the vehicle! Do it! Now!"

The Iranians were still recovering from the flash-bang's effects. Their vision was clearing, the ringing in their ears and dizziness persisted, but they definitely heard a voice.

Rahbar pushed himself up in the seat, trying to focus. He turned his head to the right, but quickly closed his eyes, feeling unbalanced. The rear seat passengers and driver were all experiencing the same distress.

"DJ, again," Grant said with a loud whisper.

James shouted, "Drop your weapons! Hands on your heads! Exit the vehicle! Now!"

There was slight movement from the Iranians in the rear seat—but not the type of movement A.T. had anticipated. The three leaned forward, then began slowly sitting upright, while still trying to focus their eyes on their attackers.

"Ken," Grant whispered, "one into the ground." Slade fired toward the road. The second explosive sound was as if someone struck a hammer against the UFs' eardrums, their agony almost unbearable.

Grant motioned with a hand. James and Kalinin started walking from their positions at the rear, pointing their Sigs toward the open windows, moving toward the vehicle at slight angles. Taking slow, deliberate steps, they finally had partial views of the men sitting closest to the rear doors.

James saw it first, the slight movement of a rifle, the barrel coming more into view. He instantly knew that the UF would have one clear shot, and it would be at Grant. James shouted, "Drop it! Drop it!"

But Izad Mohsen failed to heed the warning. James fired two consecutive rounds, one striking Mohsen's arm, shattering the humerus bone, its splinters severing the brachial artery. The second round broke ribs, penetrated lungs, blood spurted from arteries. The rifle strap had caught under the door handle, and as his bulky body started sliding sideways, the latch unlocked. He slid out of the vehicle, just as he expelled his final, long breath.

At that moment both Rahbar and Jahandar had the same thought: the attackers might be distracted for a brief moment, the moment that could give the two of them the time needed. In sudden, swift movements, they raised their pistols.

Without any hesitation, Grant and Adler fired simultaneously. Two rounds each, fired in rapid succession, slammed into the UFs' upper bodies, splintering sternums, sending shrapnel into lungs, penetrating the aorta, the remnants of bullets causing additional internal damage. Blood spurted profusely and continually. The two men slid sideways toward the console, their heads bumping against each other as the bodies continued sliding.

Grant and Adler maintained their positions, focusing their eyes on the unconscious and dying men.

Both Asadi and Zare gripped their pistols that they were keeping out of sight, but they were being more cautious than the three other men. Although, it was becoming more and more obvious that their chance of escaping was nearly zero. Zare slowly turned his head, seeing Kalinin's weapon pointed directly at him.

There was one last option for Grant to get the remaining two UFs' attention, and shouting in English, he ordered, "Out of the vehicle with hands up! This is your last warning or I promise that you will meet Allah in thirty seconds!" He glanced at his watch. "The countdown clock has started!"

Chapter 44

Inside the vehicle, the two Iranians swiveled their heads, trying to locate the attackers. They ignored the fact that English had just been spoken, which was the least of their worries. The question now was whether they would be willing to meet Allah on their own terms. Zare realized the decision would not be his, and he fixed his eyes on Asadi, waiting for that decision.

Grant knew he had the option of just blowing away the UFs and end the whole situation. But his gut was telling him he had to keep at least one of them alive. When he first had eyes on the group, there was something different about them.

Keeping his Sig pointed toward the vehicle, he held down the PTT and quietly ordered, "Back away." From there on, without a word, the men would follow his plan: he and Adler would move just beyond the rear doors; Kalinin and James would be in position protecting Grant and Adler; Slade was to the side of the tailgate, ready on Grant's signal to slam his weapon against it.

Keeping pistols trained on the UFs, the men slowly backed away, then continued sidestepping parallel to the vehicle until they were just out of the UFs' view, but prepared for any sudden movements.

Ducking low, Grant and Adler crawled next to the rear tires, then took a knee. Adler was ready to fling open the door. Grant would have to climb over the dead, heavy-set UF. They were prepared to act. They holstered their Sigs.

Slade kept eyes on Grant, waiting for the go ahead. Grant and Adler scooted closer to the doors. Grant was in a low, runner's starting position, ready to lunge over the body, ready to strike. He gave Slade the thumb's up.

Adler reached toward the door handle. Slade began pounding the tailgate. Asadi and Zare swung around, aiming their pistols toward the rear window. They both fired, shattering the glass.

Adler flung open the door, grabbed Zare's wrist, and yanked his arm back, nearly pulling the arm out of its socket. The pistol bounced off the seat, and onto the floorboards. Adler dragged Zare out of the vehicle, and slammed his body against the ground. Immediately rolling Zare on his stomach, Adler used his full weight, and jammed a knee into the small of his back. Kalinin rushed next to Zare, secured his arms behind his back, then left him lying on his stomach.

At the exact same moment Adler had made the "snatch," Grant lunged, and with a knife-edge hand, landed a blow against Asadi's neck on the vagus nerve. Asadi immediately went limp, the pistol falling onto the floorboards. Grant already had a firm grip on the shirt collar, and in one continuous motion, dragged Asadi across the seat, across the dead Mohsen, not letting go until Asadi's body landed hard on the ground. Grant came to a dead stop as he stared down at his captive.

James rushed toward Grant, ready with zip-ties, when *he* came to a standstill, seeing a green cap lying on the ground, no longer hiding the pinned up braided brown hair that now hung loosely. They were both looking down into the face of the woman they recognized as Ashira Neman.

Chapter 45

Snapping out of his surprised reaction, Grant thought, *Makes no difference, female or otherwise.* He had to search for other weapons, particularly knives. He quickly ran his hands down both her legs, finding a knife in an ankle strap. He pulled it out and handed it to James, then shouted over his shoulder, "Ken, you okay?!"

"I'm good!"

Just then, Neman started coming around, slowly opening her eyes, as her brain started functioning. She massaged her neck, trying to remember what happened. She looked up seeing someone standing over her, a stranger wearing cammies, carrying a holstered pistol. Suddenly, she remembered. She squeezed her hand as if she were still holding her weapon, but it wasn't there. Did they know who she was? Could she fake her innocence? Suddenly, she rolled over, then started scrambling to her feet, until Grant grabbed her wrist.

She cried out, "Let me go! Let me go!"

Hearing a screaming female voice, Adler was at first stunned, until noticing Grant had moved farther away from the vehicle.

"Hold onto this guy!" Adler said to Kalinin before crawling across the seat, then seeing Grant hanging onto a woman's wrist. "What the . . .?!" Adler climbed out of the vehicle, walked near James, then pressed the PTT, quietly notifying the men, "Stand-by."

Grant reached down, grabbed Neman's other wrist, then yanked her to her feet, practically lifting her off the ground. She kicked, gyrated her body, balled up her fists, trying to break free of his grasp. Holding onto both of her wrists, and using *her* fist, Grant gave her a quick pop to her jaw, just enough to get her attention. For a brief moment her face showed surprise, but then, there was only defiance.

Standing nearly a eight inches taller than her, Grant looked down at her with narrowing eyes, saying in a threatening, deep voice, "We know who you are. We've been searching for you for a very long time."

Listening to everything, Adler's brow furrowed, as he silently questioned, *What the hell is he . . .?* Then, his eyes went wide. *Holy fuck!*

She stared up at Grant, and with anger in her voice, she shouted, "And just who the hell do you *think* I am?!"

The right side of Grant's mouth curved up. "You're Mossad Agent Ashira Neman." She relaxed slightly, but he continued holding onto her because of what he was about to add. "We also know you as 'Shahbaz.'"

Obviously stunned, she shot back, "You are out of your damn mind!" She attempted to wriggle free of his grip. "Now. . let . . me . . go!"

"I'm out of *my* mind? What happened to you after your Mossad teammates were slaughtered? Were you there when the CIA agents were ambushed? And why are you here wearing an Iranian uniform, with the name 'Asadi' on a patch, and a rank of major?"

With no hesitation she shot back, "I am Mossad! I have been working undercover . . ."

"Bullshit!" Grant roared. He looked toward James. "Zip-ties!" James quickly secured Neman's wrists behind her back. Grant pushed against her shoulders, knocking her to the ground.

She landed hard on her butt, but with her hands tied behind her she had no control and continued falling onto her back. She laid there completely mystified. *How could this have happened*! *How many of my men are dead? Three,* she silently counted. *But Zare! Where is he?* The last thing she remembered was both of them firing their weapons.

Grant pressed the PTT. "We're clear. Maintain positions for now."

Neman swiveled her head, trying to locate whoever was out there. She knew she was in a critical situation with no way out. But who were these men? They had no name tags, no insignias, nothing to identify them. Speaking English meant nothing. What plans did they have for her?

"Who are you?!" she demanded angrily. She struggled to sit up, but was unsuccessful because of Grant's foot against her shoulder.

He rested a hand on his holstered pistol. "Who are we? We're the ones who found the dead CIA agent, and three dead Mossad agents at your meeting place, dead because you arranged the ambush."

"What makes you think that I . . .?!"

"Please! Don't fuckin' insult my intelligence." Grant pointed over his shoulder. "I guess you were surprised not finding the hostages. Well, we eliminated their guards, you know, the ones who perpetrated both ambushes. Your men must have surmised as much after finding dried pools of blood."

He decided it was time to put the proverbial nail or two in the coffin. Standing over her, he grabbed the front of her shirt, and jerked her closer. "Before we fly your ass outta here, I have one last surprise for you. You know the gold mine that was polluting the water, where you had the villagers doing your dirty, dangerous work? The one where you stored a helluva lot of weapons? Well, it sorta went—BOOM!" Her head snapped back from the sudden, loud sound, but she continued glaring at him with daggers in her eyes.

He gave her a shove, knocked her to the ground, then stood over her. "By the way, remember the pipeline, pump and block valve stations you thought you had control over?" He glanced at his watch. "They should be secured by friendly forces just about now." He added one final insult. "I guess your ticket for a ride home on the *Al Sham* won't be doing you a damn bit of good now."

Not waiting for any reaction, he walked away, winked at Adler, then pointed him farther from the vehicle, while he whispered to James, "Hand me the sat phone, DJ. Keep an eye on her."

As he and Adler met, Adler quietly said, "You know, you really should be on Broadway."

"It was all that prevented me from wringing her neck, Joe. Listen, collect the two pistols. Maybe stash them in plastic bags to preserve fingerprints, and mark them. Look for any other weapons and comm gear. We'll need it all."

"You got it." Leaning closer to Grant, Adler whispered, "You don't plan on her making an involuntary exit from the chopper do you, say, while it's over the Pacific?"

"No, but I can't say the thought didn't cross my mind." Grant continued walking toward Kalinin, who was guarding the bound Zare, lying face down in the dirt. "Everything good, Nick?"

"Good here. What's next?"

Grant held up the sat phone, then pressed the PTT, and got feedback from Milone, Stalley, and Novak.

Next he called the LHD, immediately hearing, "Iron-clad."

"Tango 8 here. I have orders for Condor 1."

"Lieutenants Zimmer and Daikin are here, sir. Wait one."

"Zimmer here, sir."

"Lieutenant, I need you to stand-by for further orders to fly us out. The coordinates will be the same as Condor 2's last trip. I have one other call to make which will confirm or deny whether there'll be two extra passengers, and possibly three bodies. Put body bags on-board just in case. Copy?"

"Copy."

"Stand-by in the radio room. Now, I need to have a call placed through to Langley just like last time."

"Yes, sir. Hold on."

Chapter 46

Office of Director Ray Simmons
Langley

The agent on duty at Langley answered, "00628973257."

Grant responded, "34732867 - 324538."

"Hold on."

"Carl Gordon."

"Sir, it's Grant. Is . . .?"

"He just called. He's on his way from Director Franklin's office, the deputy director of operations for the special operations group."

"Have the three agents reported in?"

"They have." Gordon looked toward the office door as it opened. "Hold on, Captain. Ray, it's Captain Stevens."

Simmons took a pen from his jacket pocket, then sat at the conference table ready to make notes on a yellow legal pad. "Captain, hold on while we add in Director Franklin."

Once Franklin was on the call, Simmons said, "We're ready, Captain. First, tell us where you are."

"Still in Aquilla."

"All right. We're listening."

"Sir, we went to the mine. The main tunnel had labeled wooden crates lined up on both sides, that extended to the back of the tunnel, nearly forty feet. There was everything from SA-7s, to RPG launchers and grenades, ammo, AK-47s, Browning pistols. I may as well tell you now, sir. We used enough C-4 to create as much damage as we could without causing the weapons to detonate, but it's likely the weapons *were* damaged." Grant opted not to mention the four Iranian bodies buried inside unless specifically questioned. "Doc took pictures before and after, but satellite or U-2 images will definitely show what's left, mostly mounds of dirt and rocks."

"Continue, Captain."

"We also found canvas sacks containing rocks with veins of gold the villagers dug out that hadn't been processed with mercury. Sir, it was my decision to turn over those sacks to the villagers, with instructions to bury them. There initially was a concern that more Iranians could show up—and they did."

"You mean you had *another* confrontation?!"

"Yes, sir, but I highly doubt it'll happen again."

Simmons' brow wrinkled. "Dare I ask, but why the doubts?"

"I'm about to answer that, sir." *Here we go,* Grant thought. He began detailing from the moment the Iranians drove onto the property, up until the up close and personal meeting with the Nissan's occupants. "We pulled two live bodies from the vehicle, and, sir, one of them was Ashira Neman."

Three different responses came from the directors: "Holy hell!" "What?!" "Jesus!"

"Say again, Captain?!" Simmons asked, obviously confounded by the news.

"Ashira Neman. It's her, sir, but . . ."

Simmons' voice deepened. "*Please* tell me she's still alive."

"Oh, *that's* affirmative. What I was about to say was there's not a doubt in my military mind that we found Shahbaz. Ashira Neman *is* Shahbaz, sir."

Simmons, Gordon and Franklin flopped back against their swivel chairs as if they'd been struck by lightning, staring at one another in disbelief.

"My God!" Gordon exclaimed. "Is it possible?!"

Simmons leaned toward the phone. "Captain, are you *absolutely* certain?!"

"I am, sir."

"And you got her to admit it?!"

"Well, she didn't deny it, but I came to the conclusion because of her reactions and bull..., uh, her answers to my questions and statements. And there were other indicators."

Simmons massaged his forehead with his fingertips. "Explain, Captain, just how you reached your conclusion."

"It never made complete sense what happened to her after the ambushes. Your agents remembered seeing her when they arrived. Then, we found the clothes in the house, which was worrisome in itself.

"Sir, I know you and the Israelis had likely questioned just how the hell the Iranians knew of the meeting, its exact location, and its attendees. That was a top secret operation. Why was she the only one who survived the Mossad slaughter?"

"That's still not sufficient, Captain. You know damn good and well there's gotta be more proof. I mean, you're accusing a Mossad agent of treason!"

"Sir, she may have *been* Mossad, she may have *been*

IDF, but I'll bet my life that she's an Iranian who had infiltrated the Israel army years ago. She was a true 'sleeper.'"

"As we suspected Shahbaz to be," Simmons quietly commented, slowly shaking his head.

"When we captured her, she was dressed in an Iranian army combat field uniform. That's why the clothes were left in the house. She wasn't attacked or raped. She voluntarily *chose* to wear it. Her uniform had a name patch showing 'Asadi' and a patch showing the rank of 'major.' I have a feeling that Asadi may be her true Iranian name. That should give you and the Israelis something to go on.

"When I confronted her about that, she had the *audacity* to claim she was working undercover. Undercover, sir! But when I told her we destroyed the mine, it were as if all the breath seemed to leave her.

"I admit, though, that I did sort of mislead her. The men with her were all officers, so it was my guess no one was left in charge in the field. She and the other four were just on an inspection tour, checking on the hostages and the weapons in the mine. And with her being captured, she'd realize there'd no longer be further communications to carry out the plan. It would all come to a standstill, so I told her the pipeline and stations were secured. Uh, and I also told her she was going to miss her ride home on the *Al Sham*."

Dead silence. Simmons, Gordon, and Franklin tried to process the intel. Simmons finally asked, "Captain, you know I have to ask, but did you or your men . . .?"

"Did we torture her? Negative, sir! Absolutely not! She's probably sore from when I yanked her outta the vehicle, and her wrists might be bruised from holding onto her. She wasn't about to give up easily, sir. And I'm sure she had leftover effects from the flash-bang, but otherwise, that was it." He opted to omit the 'pop' to her jaw.

"Have you questioned the other Iranian?"

"No, sir, not yet."

"What about pictures?"

"Doc will do that."

"The more the better. Listen, Captain, Director Franklin and I have got a helluva lot of important calls to make. Have you contacted the LHD?"

"Only to put Condor 1 on stand-by, since I needed your orders concerning Neman and her teammate. Do you want them taken to the LHD, and what would be your decision on the three Iranian bodies?" No reply. "Sir?"

"Captain, I have an idea. Stay right where you are." Simmons pressed the intercom. "Gloria, call Rachel at the White House. Secretary McKinley requested a two o'clock Sit Room meeting, but it's important that everyone who was in attendance concerning the Colombia operation be at that two o'clock. And, Gloria, stress that it's urgent." Simmons immediately made an update call to Secretary McKinley.

Chapter 47

Aquilla

While he waited, Grant motioned Adler closer, then pointed toward the male prisoner. "Joe, see what you can get outta him."

"Think it's safe for the villagers to relax?"

"It should be, but I still want Vince and Mike to stay on alert. Wait, Joe. Unless he hasn't already, have Doc take pictures of the shed and sacks, and maybe Vince can get some villagers' names."

"You mean in case we need witnesses?" Grant nodded. Adler started walking away, then stopped. "I take it we didn't get orders from Langley."

"Not yet, probably because they were in shock."

Adler contacted Milone and Novak while he walked toward Kalinin who was guarding the Iranian.

"What's happening?" Kalinin asked. Adler quietly relayed the little he knew.

Grant looked toward Neman, just as he noticed James trying to get his attention. James pointed at her, then toward the vehicle. Grant shook his head. He wanted her to stay where she was, hoping to keep her uncomfortable, giving her quiet time to think about her fate. But his impression of her was that she'd have no remorse for her past, her actions, her orders to have people killed, their lives destroyed. *She deserves everything she's gonna get.*

He rested the sat phone against his shoulder while reviewing his statements to Simmons, then began silently questioning whether Neman would have the ability to possibly bluff her way out of her dire situation. He was more than positive who she really was, but would it be her word against his? Who would the Israelis believe? Who would CIA believe? He and probably his men would face grilling at their debriefing, maybe one of the toughest in their careers.

Fifteen minutes had passed when Grant heard Simmons voice. "Captain?"

"Yes, sir?"

"What I'm about to tell you means you and your men will have to sit tight until dark. And, Captain, the decision has already been made."

"Understood."

"Secretary McKinley spoke with Secretary Daniels and Mossad Director Chaikin. I don't think I need to tell you what their reactions were hearing the news. Anyway, to keep this short, Director Chaikin contacted the prime minister. Everyone has agreed with our proposal, which is, Ambassador Ben-Ari and five of his security men will depart Bogotá at two o'clock, your time. The ambassador's private jet will arrive in Palmira around three. They'll drive to the village, then transport Neman and her teammate back to the aircraft for the direct flight to Israel. Understood?"

"Understood, sir. Truthfully, it'll be a relief to have them off our hands. But what about the three bodies?"

"I didn't get an answer on that, but I don't believe the decision will be left with you."

"Glad to hear that. Sir, we collected their weapons and comm gear. Do you want us to . . ."

"Turn everything over to the ambassador."

"Very well, sir."

"As a side note, Captain, Secretary McKinley and SecDef Daniels were preparing to contact Colombia's Defense Minister Pedro Mendoza. We expect his army will begin striking the Quds Force along the pipeline."

"Great news, sir! When we're finished here, I'll contact the LHD . . ."

"Not necessary. Secretaries Canon and Daniels had made tentative arrangements. Those will be firmed up now that you've reported in. The CO is being notified and will advise Condor 1's crew that they'll fly you and your men from Aquilla directly to a carrier on station in the Caribbean, then on to Gitmo. I assume the pilots will contact you before departing the ship."

"Very well, sir. Sir, what about Agent Kaufman?"

Director Franklin responded, "He didn't have any family, and since he was former Navy, the CO will have him buried at sea."

Grant quietly responded, "That's befitting for all he's done, sir."

"Yes, yes it is," Franklin said, clearing his throat.

Grant made a mental note for he and his men to pay their respects at Langley, once Kaufman's star had been carved into the marble of the Memorial Wall.

"Sir, has a decision been made regarding the bodies of the Mossad agents?"

"Not yet. Listen, Captain, it seems I've been giving you a helluva lot of 'not yets' and 'I don't knows.'"

"But I understand, sir."

"Well, let me head off a question you're bound to be asking about the *Al Sham*. She's still due to anchor

tonight, then dock a.m. tomorrow. From intercepts between the *Al Sham* and port officials, once she's off-
loaded her cargo, she'll be heading back to Syria, without
additional passengers."

"You mean the passengers I suggested?"

"We believe you were correct. But in any case, as of
now, there won't be any reason to board her."

Grant arched an eyebrow. "Sir, are you *expecting* a
reason?"

Simmons ignored the question, and instead ordered,
"You and your men will board Condor 1 this evening.
Understood?"

"Yes, sir."

"All right. Once you're home, you'll be contacted
with the date and time for your debriefing. And, Captain,
to you and your men, good job, and safe journey."

"Thank you, Mr. Director."

Grant hooked the phone on his belt, while reviewing
the conversation, wondering what the hell was going on
with the *Al Sham*. Was Simmons waiting for intercepts?
If the Quds in the field were expecting orders from Neman and none came, would they take it upon themselves
and bail from the country via the cargo ship, or would
they head into Venezuela? Had he been wrong in thinking that there weren't more Iranian officers in the field,
who would pick up the reins if they didn't hear from her?
Maybe those concerns no longer mattered, since the
Colombians were expected to root out the guerrilla
groups and Quds Force. But considering the length of
the pipeline and number of stations spread out for miles,
how long would it take?

There was one way to shorten the time for such a search: satellite images. But would Simmons be willing to turn over such specific details? *Hell,* Grant thought, *every country knows about spy satellites, and the Colombians are no different.* He had to believe Simmons would make that decision. It was the quickest way to stop the Iranians' threat.

"Take no prisoners," Grant mumbled.

"Say what?" Adler asked, walking up behind him.

"Nothing. We got our orders. We're gonna have to plant our asses here until dark."

"Oh joy," Adler said, shaking his head. "And the reason for our asses remaining?"

Grant pressed the PTT. "Listen up. We've got orders to remain here until dark." He gave his men complete details on his conversation with Simmons. No questions were asked. "Okay, in the meantime, we've got things to do. Mike, set up just below us. Vince, is it quiet by you and Doc?"

"Affirm. I got several names just as LT requested."

"Good. Tell everyone there's another vehicle coming late this afternoon, and assure them they shouldn't worry."

"Roger."

"Doc, need you here to take pictures."

"On my way."

Grant glanced at Neman, then waved Slade toward him. "Ken, I wanna make her and her buddy a touch more uncomfortable. When Doc's finished taking pictures, help DJ and Nick secure them two to a tree, then blindfold them."

Slade slapped a hand against his mouth, then asked, "What about some duct tape?"

"Sure. Knock yourself out." Seeing Stalley hustling toward the Nissan, Grant said, "C'mon, Joe. Let's look that vehicle over one last time."

Chapter 48

Tel Aviv

Sitting in a leather chair in his office, Mossad Director Chaikin reviewed in his mind the news from the Americans. *There have been, and there always will be traitors to any country—but a Mossad agent? And not just a traitor—but an Iranian!*

Somehow Neman had first infiltrated the IDF, and then Mossad. Had she always been truthful during her debriefings after returning from top secret missions? She had experienced all the training, knew all the weapons, was a crack shot with a pistol and rifle, and she was an expert at using her feminine wiles on many unsuspecting targets.

It seems that this time she *was the unsuspecting target,* Chaikin thought, with some satisfaction.

The ambassador's plane will not be arriving in Tel Aviv until tomorrow morning, which would be enough time to speak with the department heads, and completely inform them of the . . . what? Disgrace? Embarrassment? Fear it could happen again? How to prevent it from happening again? And perhaps the most looming question: what to do about or with Neman? Right now there was one known fact: the name Neman had on her Iranian uniform—Asadi. His people were already investigating.

Then there was the matter of three dead Mossad agents aboard an American ship, along with four live Iranians. Arrangements to bring the agents' bodies home had been decided on. Transporting the Iranians with his agents galled him to no end, but there was no other way. *Were they important enough to use as leverage, or a trade?* Perhaps not those four, but the man captured with Neman might prove to be invaluable. Could he be persuaded to turn against her, if she truly worked for Iran?

But maybe he was getting ahead of himself. So far only one side of the story had been told, and that was not even the entire story. He would call Secretary McKinley, or better still, Director Simmons. *Then, perhaps if I am still unsatisfied, I will request a debriefing with the men who found and accused her. But why would those men tell untruths? What reason would they have? And yet, once she and the other four were captured, all activity along the pipeline had ceased.* His doubts began to subside. He glanced at his watch, then walked to the corner window overlooking the city. *Perhaps I will wait and talk with the ambassador before making any calls to the U.S., and hope I get an answer about the name 'Asadi.'*

"In the meantime . . ." He went to the desk, and looked up the number for the military advocate general.

*

Aquilla
1715 Hours

The sun was just beginning to set, when Novak reported, "Eyes on two vehicles, a sedan and panel van."

Grant stepped from behind the Nissan. "DJ, on my

signal contact *Ironclad*, requesting Condor 1 pick us up."

"Roger, boss!"

"Ken, Nick, ready our departing guests. Remove only the duct tape just before you head out, but don't rip it off. I'll signal when to bring them. Doc, I want you to take pictures as our guests are turned over to the ambas- sador. You've gotta do it covertly, Doc. Got it?"

"Got it," Stalley answered, attaching the telephoto lens.

"Mike, remain in position for now."

"Roger."

"Are we being a bit paranoid?" Adler kiddingly ques- tioned, jabbing Grant with an elbow.

"Damn right, Joe. C'mon." The two walked along the road, waiting for Novak's final report.

Within a minute they heard his voice in their ear- pieces. "Black Renault sedan, driver, one passenger, rear seat. Second vehicle, white Renault panel van; only dri- ver and front passenger visible."

As the vehicles started slowing, Grant and Adler crossed the road. Grant did a quick scan of the area, un- able to locate Stalley.

The sedan stopped directly in front of them, with the van nearly bumper to bumper behind it. Four men exited the van, all wearing black T-shirts, black pants, bullet- resistants vests, and shoulder holsters, their weapons par- tially concealed by black windbreakers.

The driver of the sedan opened the right rear door. Ambassador Ben-Ari stepped from the sedan, buttoning his black suit jacket as he did.

Grant extended a hand. "Mr. Ambassador, I'm Grant

Stevens, sir."

Ben-Ari grasped Grant's hand firmly. "Captain Stevens, these are unusual circumstances for us to be meeting."

"Yes, sir, they are." Grant motioned toward Adler. "Sir, this is Lieutenant Adler." The two shook hands. Grant said, "Mr. Ambassador, you probably don't have much time, so, unless you have questions for us, I'll turn the prisoners over to you."

Ben-Ari nodded. "We will gladly accept them."

Grant pressed the PTT. "Okay, Ken, Nick."

As Slade and Kalinin led the two, Grant directed Ben-Ari's attention to the Nissan. "Sir, that was their vehicle. I was told you would be handling it and the three dead inside."

"Yes. We will handle that when we leave. I assume there is a key?"

"It's still in the ignition. Sir, we weren't sure what your plans were, so we put the three bodies in the rear seat."

As Slade and Kalinin approached, two of the security men from the van took charge of the blindfolded prisoners, while the other two men stood by the open rear panel doors.

Zare constantly gyrated his body, digging his heels into the ground. Frantically trying to break free, he shouted, "No! N o o o!" One of the security men by the van ran to assist, and grabbing Zare's other arm, they dragged him toward the open rear doors.

Once in the van, his wrists remained secured with the zip-ties. Legcuffs were fastened around his ankles, the chain between the cuffs already shortened making it impossible to even walk.

Having heard the sound of vehicles approaching, Neman had to assume that she and Zare were being handed over to unknowns. As she was being led toward the rear of the van, her voice rose, "Who are you?! Where are you taking us?!" Silence. She quickly decided to take a different approach, and screamed at the top of her lungs, "They have told you lies about me! Lies! You must give me a chance to speak, to explain! You must! You must believe me!"

Grant's stomach tightened. *I* knew *it.*

Ignoring her constant, loud prattle, the security men lifted her into the van, then secured her the same as Zare. Legcuffs and zip-ties were rechecked on both prisoners. The security men took seats opposite one another, closer to the cab. The doors closed, then were locked. The driver slid behind the steering wheel, while the other man went to the ambassador. "Prisoners are secured, sir. We left the blindfolds in place."

"Good." Ben-Ari looked toward the van, hearing Neman proclaiming her innocence. Ignoring the annoying sound, he pointed the security man to the Nissan. "The key is in the ignition. I will be ready in a moment."

"Just a minute," Grant said, looking toward the security man. "We left their comm gear and weapons in the vehicle. Both *their* pistols are in marked plastic bags."

The security man removed a satchel from the trunk, then jogged to the Nissan, carrying a second smaller satchel. He glanced at the three bodies, then collected the comm gear and weapons. Once finished, he started the engine, then waited.

Extending a hand toward Grant first, then Adler, Ben-Ari said, "It is with sincere appreciation that we thank all of you for what you have done."

"Thank you, sir. But we'd like to extend our sympathies for the loss of your agents. I'm sure they were very fine men."

"Thank you, Captain." Ben-Ari got in the vehicle, the door closed, then the engine started. The driver made a K-turn, then proceeded east, with the van following closely, and the Nissan not far behind.

Once the vehicles were out of view, Grant breathed a sigh. "Okay, Joe, let's get our gear. DJ, contact the chopper!"

"Aye, aye, *sir*!" James shouted.

Grant looked toward Novak's position. "Mike, come on in!" Novak got to his feet, then hurried toward his teammates. But as he started to pass, Grant stopped him. "Mike, you wanna talk about anything? You know I'm always ready to listen."

"I know, boss. And I know what you're referring to, but what came over me . . . well, I just don't know. It's never happened before. And I've seen a helluva lot worse damage that I've personally caused." He lowered his eyes.

Grant laid a hand on his shoulder. "Mike, I can't and won't try to minimize what you experienced, what you felt at that moment. You alone have to deal with it. I know you realize that your duties, abilities, have also saved lives, Mike, and mostly ours. Each of us has had something that'll never be erased from our minds. The pictures will always be there. All we can do is . . . go on.

"Look, Mike, you're a helluva integral part of this Team, and you're more than just a teammate. You're our brother. But if you need to take a break, or anything beyond that, you know all of us will understand, and we'll stand by your decision."

"I know, boss." Slight creases appeared at the corners of Novak's blue eyes, as he smiled and waved an arm overhead. "How could I give all this up?!"

Grant lightly slapped his arm. "Okay, Mike. Go join your 'brothers.'"

Adler had been watching the two, and finally stepped closer to Grant. "Was that your talk?"

"Yeah, I think he's okay. It was just one of those shit moments he had to deal with back at the mine."

"So he's still our 'sniper boy'?"

"He is." Grant waved Stalley toward him. "Did you snap some good ones, Doc?"

"Nobody smiled, but I think the pictures will do the job, boss."

"Good. C'mon. Let's get our gear ready."

*

Ten minutes after the men finished carrying their gear to the edge of the field, a loud explosion made them swing around, and drop to the ground, their weapons already in their hands.

"What the . . .?" Adler bellowed.

With weapons pointed straight ahead, they cautiously walked toward the road, finally seeing flames and black smoke rising above the jungle floor. Remaining on alert, they listened for any other sound, watched for any vehicles. Nothing.

Grant slowly stood, holstering his Sig. "The Nissan," he quietly said.

"What?! You think they blew it up?!" Kalinin asked, stunned.

"I don't know what else it could've been, Nick. Once we're aboard the chopper, I'll ask Lieutenant Zimmer to swing over that way."

Noticing some of the villagers cautiously walking toward the road, looking in the direction of the explosion, Grant said, "Vince, see what you can do about reassuring them that they should be safe from now on. Tell them we'll be on our way shortly. C'mon, guys, let's go shake some hands. We've put these folks through enough."

*

It was nearly dark when James answered the call. "This is Tango 8. Over."

Lieutenant Daikin responded, "Tango 8, this is Condor 1! We are on course, five miles out. Any updates? Over."

"Negative, Condor 1. We are prepared for departure. Will signal with red light. Over."

"Copy that. See you in a few. Condor 1, out."

A.T., ensuring that their holsters' restrainers were secured over their pistols, they hooked straps of their rucksacks on their shoulders, then held their MP5s, Slade his shotgun, Novak his rifle.

Even though he didn't have on his NVGs, Grant was still prepared to use the pen light's red light to signal the chopper, certain Condor 1 would have its IR searchlight on.

"Here it comes," Grant said, hearing the familiar sound. He turned on the pen light, then started waving it overhead.

Dust and debris obliterated the LZ as Condor 1 descended, then touched down.

"Let's go!" Grant ordered. Within a couple of minutes, the men were on-board. The crew chief helped secure their gear. Grant leaned in toward the cockpit, offering a hand to both pilots. "Gentlemen, it's good to see you, believe me!"

Zimmer and Daikin both smiled, but before either could comment, Grant asked, "Did you see black smoke east of here during your approach?"

"We did, sir, maybe two klicks."

"That's it. Listen, I'd like you to do a quick flyover. I'm looking for a burned out vehicle."

"Yes, sir." Zimmer engaged the blades, and slowly lifted the collective. Engines roared, as Condor 1 rose, briefly hovered, then Zimmer deftly moved the cyclic, adjusted a pedal, and brought the chopper on its easterly heading.

Grant looked through the windshield, as his men crawled closer to the open cargo bay door. Stalley had the camera ready.

"There, sir!" Daikin pointed straight ahead.

"That's gotta be it," Grant said.

Zimmer adjusted the cyclic. As the chopper approached the area, he brought it to within thirty feet above the ground, lightly depressed the right pedal, causing the tail to slowly start moving left. Then, he slowly moved the cyclic left, and gradually, the chopper started circling the smoldering, burned-out Nissan.

"Damn," Grant mumbled, looking down at a completely destroyed vehicle, and only imagining what was left of the bodies. *Probably not a helluva lot.*

"Sir," Zimmer called loudly above the engine noise, "if you want, I can land."

"Not necessary, Lieutenant. I got my answer." Grant turned toward the cargo bay. "Doc?!" Stalley held up the camera, and gave an okay sign. "Okay, Lieutenant, thanks. You can get us outta here now."

"Yes, sir. Sir, we're gonna be flying NOE until we reach the coast."

Signaling with a thumb's up, Grant joined his men sitting on the deck. "We're going NOE, guys!"

The crew chief pulled the cargo bay door closed, and with his NVGs lowered, he assumed his position behind the cockpit, near the open window, and opposite the gunner.

Condor 1's nose dipped, then picked up speed, heading west.

Adler leaned toward Grant. "You do know that it was more than just a damn grenade that destroyed that Nissan! Did you see that security guy carrying a small satchel?" Grant nodded, as Adler added, "Somebody had bomb-making experience!"

"No doubt, Joe."

"By the way," Adler said, handing Grant a roast beef

sandwich. "Compliments of the crew, and there's some hot coffee. Guess we'd better hold off on the coffee until we stop this roller coaster ride. These guys must think they're on a bombing run!"

Chapter 49

Guantanamo Bay
Monday
0030 Hours

Twenty-seven thousand pounds of fuel were already in the *Herc's* tanks. But in case of an unknown situation, Scott Mullins gave Matt Garrett the frequency and call sign of a refueling tanker.

A preflight inspection, then a run through of the pre-flight checklist were all that was needed before takeoff—and the eight men of A.T. For Matt Garrett and Rob Draper, takeoff time was currently a question.

A few hours earlier, while they were having dinner at the Windjammer, a breaking TV news story reported Colombian forces were fighting guerrilla's somewhere along a major pipeline. Videos and other details had not been made available. Garrett and Draper immediately stopped eating, focusing on the report. They were probably the only ones in the dining room who were partially aware of the circumstances that most likely led up to the fighting.

Inside the *Herc's* cargo bay, stretched out on orange jump seats across from one another, Garrett and Draper were wide awake, waiting for word on their teammates.

"Captain Garrett, sir!" Petty Office Cardone called, standing at the foot of the *Herc's* lowered ramp.

Garrett sat up and waved the petty officer into the cargo bay. "Any word?"

283

"Yes, sir. Condor 1's fifteen minutes out, sir. It's been given clearance to land on helo pad two. That'd be straight ahead of your aircraft, sir, just this side of the runway."

"All right. Thanks, petty officer."

Cardone snapped a salute then as he started to leave, Garrett called, "Wait. Was there any request for medical services?"

The young petty officer wrinkled up his face. "Medical? Uh, nothing was mentioned, sir."

"All right. That's all." Cardone hurried to the duty vehicle, then drove off.

"Phew! Damn," Garrett said.

"Yeah, you said it," Draper added, sitting up, and blowing out a long breath, obviously relieved. "Matt, maybe I should pick up some extra food and drinks."

"Good idea, Rob." Garrett took some bills from his wallet. "Here. This should do it."

"Matt, I was gonna . . ."

"I know. Don't worry about it. You get it next time, and we both know there'll sure as hell be a next time," Garrett said smiling. Draper hurried down the ramp, then jogged toward the building.

Garrett left the cargo bay, then walked around the wing, and stopped in front of the *Herc*. Shoving his hands into his pants pockets, he stared across the airfield and pitch black Caribbean. The moon had disappeared below the horizon. Now, where sea met sky it was nearly impossible to see the separation between the two.

He squinted as he tried focusing on a light not far above the south southwest horizon. "That's gotta be it."

*

Aboard Condor 1

Condor 1's crew chief confirmed with Daikin, then leaned toward Grant, "Sir, we're approaching Gitmo! Expected landing in five!" he signaled displaying five fingers.

Grant gave a thumb's up, then looked at his men, who had heard the announcement, and with their voices deep and in unison, they shouted, "Hooyah!"

Soon after, they heard a sudden change in the turboshaft engines, felt the deceleration, and a change in the angle. Condor 1 hovered briefly, then settled onto helo pad two. The crew chief pushed open the cargo bay door, then jumped out and shoved the wheel chocks behind the wheels.

Grant and his men were already on their feet, hoisting rucksacks onto their backs, hooking weapon straps on their shoulders. Grant leaned into the cockpit, offering a hand to Zimmer and Daikin. "Gentlemen, you've all gone above and beyond. Thanks again, from each of us."

"Our pleasure again, sir," Zimmer smiled.

"Will you all be overnighting here?"

"Yes, sir."

"I don't know if we'll be departing immediately, but if not, maybe we can treat all of you to breakfast. No guarantees, but if you see the *Herc* still parked, stop by. Okay?"

"Yes, sir, we will."

"Have a good night, gentlemen." Grant shook hands with the gunner and crew chief, then jumped from the cargo bay, meeting his men who were waiting alongside the chopper.

"Matt's over there," Adler said, tilting his head.

As A.T. walked toward the *Herc,* Garrett snapped a salute as he started toward them. "Welcome back, guys!" he smiled. He reached for Grant's hand, holding onto it with a firm grip. "So, how'd it go? No. Wait. Fill us in during the flight home."

"Sure, Matt." Halfway up the ramp, Grant stopped and turned toward Garrett. "Hey, do you know something that we don't? When *do* we leave?" Hearing that, Adler and the rest of A.T. came to a standstill.

"Rob and I saw a brief TV news report about what was happening down there. The Colombians were attacking guerrilla groups along a pipeline. We got a call from Langley not long after. We were ordered to depart as soon as you landed."

"I guess I shouldn't be surprised from either report," Grant said, laying down his gear, then tossing his helmet onto the jump seat.

"There's more."

"Yeah, the debriefing. When?"

"Tomorrow, 1400, Langley. The whole Team's been invited."

"No rest for the weary," Adler commented, flopping down on a seat.

"Hey!" Draper shouted hurrying up the ramp, carrying two large shopping bags. He put the bags on a seat then went around and shook each man's hand.

"I smell fried chicken," Adler said sniffing the air.

"Rob, is there enough to invite the chopper crew to join in?" Grant asked.

"I'd say so, Grant. Besides chicken and biscuits there are enough sub sandwiches. We've got drinks in the cooler."

"DJ," Grant said, "see if they've finished post-flight check. Invite them over." James hustled away. Grant added, "Whether they join us or not, what say we eat first, then head home. Screw Langley's order."

A combined "Hooyah!" echoed throughout the *Herc.*

A sound of boots pounding on the ramp got every-one's attention, as James called out, "Look who I found!"

Grant smiled and greeted the chopper crew. "Wel-come aboard! C'mon. Let's eat."

At 0145, Garrett steered the *Herc* onto the end of Runway 21, immediately receiving clearance from the control tower. With brakes full on, he ran up the engines to full revs, then released the brakes, and opened the throttle completely. The *Herc* started its takeoff roll. Draper kept his eyes on the speed indicator, calling out the speed. Garrett continued advancing the throttles, un-til the engines stabilized at forty-five percent, when he accelerated them to takeoff thrust. Reaching Vr (rotation speed), and once the runway was clear, the nose gear and landing gear were retracted. Making a slow, wide left turn, he brought the aircraft around in almost a half cir-cle, bringing its heading to 354°, continuing to climb to an altitude of 24,000 feet. In about three and a half hours, Team A.T. would be home.

Chapter 50

Washington, D.C.
Monday
0715 Hours

The apartment door closed. Grant leaned back against it, still wearing his cammies. He and his men had slept a couple of hours on the *Herc.* They took time at Eagle 8 to clean their weapons before hauling ass for home.

He blew out a breath as he was walking to the kitchen, then took an unopened bottle of ice cold milk from the fridge. Not even pouring it in a glass, he started drinking straight from the bottle as he walked to the living room window, and opened the blinds. The sun had been up for over an hour. *Back to normal,* he thought. *Back to lots of concrete, and no jungle.*

He glanced at his watch while calculating the time he had to make a couple of calls, shower, then hit the sack for at least two hours before Adler showed up and they left for Langley. *Time to get moving, Stevens.*

Gulping down the last mouthfuls of milk, he sat on the couch, pressed the speed dial number, and as he waited, he untied his boots.

"Hello?"

"Hi, Alexandra."

"Oh, my goodness! Grant! Thank God! I'm so happy you're home."

"Yeah, so am I," he laughed.

"When will we see you? You must come for dinner,

you, Joe, and Nicolai."

"I'll have to get back to you on that, Alexandra. But we will, I promise."

"All right. Grigori is standing right here."

"My friend! My friend! You are safe," Moshenko said expressing his relief.

"Yeah, we all made it home in decent shape, Grigori."

"That is good to know. But I can hear it in your voice that you are very tired."

"That's the way it goes, my friend. We've still got our debriefing this afternoon."

"I guess it is too early for you to call Luke."

"I'll call him in an hour or so. Look, Grigori, I'm gonna get going. I still haven't showered. I'll try to catch some Zs before the debrief. I'll call you tonight, okay?"

"Of course. You rest. I will talk with you later."

*

Grant rested a hand against the tile surface, letting hot water beat against his shoulders, while he thought about the upcoming debriefing. How much more had CIA learned since the Team left Colombia? Garrett said the news had only briefly reported the fighting along the pipeline. *CIA had to have a helluva lot more by now.*

But aside from that, what had Israel, and specifically the Mossad, decided about Neman? *Maybe it's still too early, if the ambassador's plane hasn't arrived in Tel Aviv.*

He wiped water from his face as he smiled and wondered how many hours Neman had howled during the flight, continuing to proclaim her innocence. She had masterfully avoided capture for so long, and possibly because intel agencies were always looking for a man. As much as he hated to, he had to give kudos to Iran for managing to keep that a deep, dark secret, even more so because of their usual low regard for women. Somehow, she -- they -- managed to pull it off.

Thinking back on the ambassador's security team, he wondered if any of them were Mossad on special assignment, who would've had explosives training. And it would only take one agent to G2 Neman. The long fifteen hour flight would be more than enough time to question her and her Iranian associate.

He ducked his head out from under the water, hearing the phone ringing. Grabbing a towel, he wrapped it around himself, then hustled to the living room while brushing wet strands of hair from his forehead. "Stevens."

"Oh, sir, you're home!"

"Hey, Luke! Yeah, got in almost an hour ago. I didn't call 'cause I didn't think you'd be up this early. Obviously, I was wrong."

"I'm happy you're home safe, sir."

"Me, too," Grant laughed. "Hey, tell me about the guys in your platoon?"

"They're a great bunch, from our platoon commander right on down to me." Grant detected a smile in his son's voice, making him smile. They talked for another thirty minutes, mostly about Luke's continued training, until Grant asked, "Have you spoken with your mom?"

"A few days ago. She and Blake are settled into their

new home. She seems to like Seattle. She wants me to visit."

"You know you should."

"Sure, but I wanna come see you first, if that's possible."

"Well, is there any chance you can take some leave in the next couple of weeks?"

"I was waiting until I heard from you, but I've already got a tentative okay."

"All right. You give me a firm date, and I'll make the reservations." He glanced at his submariner. "Luke, it always seems I'm short on time, but I've got another call to make, then I wanna get a couple hours of Zs before our 1400 debriefing, which will probably last at least a few hours. Leave a message if I'm not here or try catching me at Eagle 8."

"Will do, sir, and welcome home."

"Thanks, Luke. I'll be talking with you soon." As he walked back to the shower, he questioned for the umpteenth time how he was going to react when his kid went on his first mission. And that would happen before he knew it.

He stepped into the shower, when he thought, *Maybe I should call Claudia.* It wasn't a conversation he wanted to deal with before the debriefing. *I'll call her tonight and ask if I can stop by her apartment. A face to face would be better, no matter what the outcome.*

Chapter 51

CIA
Langley
Monday
1340 Hours

Adler and Slade, each driving one of the Chevy SUVs, stopped their vehicles at the security guard station at Langley. IDs were presented, each name checked off, visitor badges distributed, then they were waved ahead.

Dressed in suits, with CIA visitor badges clipped to their jacket lapels, the ten men of Team A.T. walked into the lobby fifteen minutes early. Gathering by the Memorial Wall, they waited for their escort.

"Guess we'll be back to pay our respects once Agent Kaufman's star has been carved,"Adler said quietly,

Grant nodded, while looking at the star he knew represented his friend, and Scott Mullins' brother, Tony.

They heard heels clicking on the marble tile floor, and then the voice of Simmons' secretary, Gloria. "Captain Stevens?"

"Yes, ma'am."

"Will you and your men follow me, please?"

As they were walking down the hallway, Grant handed her rolls of film, requesting they be developed then delivered to the conference room.

Inside the brightly lit room were two long tables arranged end to end along one wall. A total of eight black swivel chairs were behind the tables. Opposite those tables, and about twelve feet away, were two tables, seating ten.

Grant's first thought when he walked in was it reminded him of the first time he testified in front of a Congressional committee. Sliding his hands into his pants pockets, he cast his eyes downward. *Is this gonna be a debriefing, or a G2?* He and his men had nothing to hide.

"Captain."

Grant turned. "Mr. Secretary, it's good to see you, sir."

Secretary of Defense Daniels reached for Grant's hand. "And you, Captain." Daniels looked at the men of A.T. who were standing close by. "I don't believe I've had the pleasure of meeting all of you gentlemen." He shook each man's hand, as they introduced themselves, then, "We're all eager to hear your report on Colombia."

"And we're eager to tell it, sir," Grant said. "It was certainly a surprising mission."

"I assume you mean learning that Neman was Shahbaz."

"Absolutely, Mr. Secretary. She was probably the perfect sleeper agent."

"That she was. I don't know if we'll ever find out how they pulled it off, but if anyone does, it'll be the Israelis."

Being led by Director Simmons, the remaining attendees walked in: Secretary of the Navy Canon; Secretary of State McKinley; National Security Advisor Hillman; Deputy Directors Franklin and Gordon; NSA Director

Prescott.

Simmons walked toward Grant and his men. "Captain, men, welcome back."

Grant responded, "Thank you, sir."

Simmons motioned to a man next to him. "Captain, this is Secretary of State McKinley."

Grant offered a hand. "It's a pleasure, sir."

"And you, Captain."

Handshakes and greetings continued, until Simmons finally said, "Gentlemen, let's begin."

"Sir," Grant said quietly, "can you tell me if you've had any luck with the Iranian name on Neman's uniform?"

Simmons shook his head. "Net yet, but we and the Israelis are working hard on it."

Once everyone was seated, Simmons opened a file folder. "Captain, all of us here have reviewed and compared notes from your phone calls, and our conversations with Director Franklin's men. But, we'd still like you to begin with your findings at your original target, the meeting house. We'll be sure to interrupt if something isn't clear. And if any of your men wish to contribute, they may do so. All right, go ahead."

*

Nearly two hours later, Grant and his men had detailed every aspect of the mission up until the destruction of the Nissan. Then, Grant said, "The Israeli ambassador and his men departed the area in the sedan. Neman and her associate were in the van. One of the security men drove the Nissan from the property. About ten minutes later an explosion occurred in the direction they'd driven.

"When Condor 1 arrived, both pilots verified they saw the smoke. I requested that we be flown over the area. The Nissan was still burning, totally destroyed. Lieutenant Zimmer offered to land for us to inspect it, but I didn't see any reason to, so I requested we head out.

"Sirs, Lieutenant Adler, who's former EOD, concluded that the explosion could not have been caused by a grenade. For the amount of destruction, someone had to have had experience with explosives."

Secretary Daniels asked, "Captain, if I understood you, you decided *not* to inspect the vehicle?"

"That's correct, sir. The Iranians inside were already dead. That was fact. What else could've been done with the bodies? I guess if I were in the ambassador's place, I would've made the same decision, but I'm sure he'll be questioned by the prime minister and the Mossad director."

Simmons noticed a flashing yellow light on the silenced phone. "Excuse me." The call was very brief. He hung up, just as the conference door opened, and someone rolled in a projector, setting it at the far end of the room. Simmons explained, "Those are your pictures from the mission, Captain. It would've taken too long to pass them around, so we had the films converted to slides. Carl, would you operate the projector?" Everyone swiveled around their chairs, as Gordon turned on the projector, and Simmons commented, "We'll speak up if we have questions."

Most of the images were self-explanatory. Grant was

asked to identify individuals, both alive and dead, from the meeting place and Aquilla, and if not by name, then by the associated group. He breathed a quiet sigh, after noticing Stalley hadn't taken pictures of the two men Novak eliminated at the mine. *Thanks, Doc,* he silently thought.

Grant gave detailed explanations on the interior of the mine, and location of the weapons. Simmons interrupted briefly, noting sat images in the folders showed the exterior aftermath of the explosion.

The next group of pictures were probably the most highly anticipated—the capture of Ashira Neman. Simmons requested that Grant describe each, no matter how graphic.

Through several slides, Grant was the only one who had spoken, until a picture of Neman appeared, showing her wearing an Iranian uniform, and the name patch of 'Asadi.'

Daniels made an observation on the unkempt condition of Neman's uniform and hair. "Can we assume she didn't arrive in that condition, Captain?"

Grant thought, *Uh-oh, here we go.* "She didn't, sir. We tried three times to get them outta the vehicle voluntarily. They resisted. Joe dragged out her associate, and I dragged her out. I will admit, sir, that I used some force in order to get her out, so she hit the ground pretty hard. Then as she regained her senses, she attempted to escape by rolling across the dirt and grass. That's when I grabbed her, and we secured her wrists, sir."

Secretary McKinley asked, "Did you threaten her, in any way?"

"Absolutely *not*, sir, neither did my men. I only confronted her with the facts we had, as in the ambushes that killed the Mossad agents and Agent Kaufman, the villagers working the mine, the water being polluted with mercury. Oh, I did happen to mention that she was going to miss her ride home on the *Al Sham*. That's what I did, sir."

"And did she deny everything?" McKinley asked.

"Of course she did, sir."

"And yet, you're positive she's Shahbaz."

"Yes, sir. I am. While her three men were inspecting the house, she stood outside the Nissan, unrestrained. They appeared to be reporting to her when they finished that inspection.

"Sir, no disrespect intended, but you weren't there confronting her, seeing her reactions, especially when she wanted me to believe that her Iranian uniform meant she was working undercover."

McKinley just nodded, and leaned back against his chair, continuing to watch Grant, who had a certain fire in his eyes.

The button on the phone blinked again. "Yes?" Simmons answered perturbed. He listened, and then asked, "Was that from an intercept? Okay, what else." Whatever was said definitely got Simmons' attention. "Are they absolutely positive?" Again he listened. "All right, but I want our own confirmation." He hung up, dropped his pen on the note pad, then announced, "Okay, first. We intercepted a transmission from within the Colombian government's offices stating that Miguel Montoya, the assistant minister of security, was arrested. That's all I'll say for now." Simmons specifically set his eyes on Grant. "That second part of the call confirmed that the Israelis discovered a first name that goes along with 'Asadi.' It's 'Tannaz' and it's a female name. And it belongs to Ashira Neman—positively."

Grant rolled his chair back, disbelieving but relieved. His men looked at him, then at each other, finally breaking into smiles.

"No comments, Captain?" Simmons asked with a hint of a smile.

"No, sir, but I do have a question."

"Go ahead."

"Has the ambassador's plane arrived in Tel Aviv?"

"About ten this morning, our time. I assume your question has to do with her G2. The answer is they haven't revealed that yet, and they haven't said where she and her teammate are being held. That's all I can tell you for now."

"Understood, sir."

Everyone in the room finally settled down. Grant's attention was again drawn to the image on the screen. "Sir, I think there are one or two more images remaining. I'll have another question or two once they're shown." Simmons motioned to Gordon.

Grant addressed all the men on the panel. "Sirs, those are the bags of rocks with veins of gold the villagers manually dug from the tunnel. Will they be allowed to keep them? Does the Colombian government have to know?" He immediately requested the next slide. The image filled the screen, causing quiet murmurs, but mostly smiles. "Those are a majority of the villagers, both young and old, who dug out those rocks, sirs, and whose lives have been affected not only by the Iranians, but I guess somewhat by us. We don't know how many of them might already be experiencing symptoms from the mercury they handled, drank, washed in. Will anything be done to help them, and if so, by whom? It sure won't be the Iranians. I believe that's all, sirs."

Gordon turned on the overhead lights, bringing into view the expression on Simmons' face and each man sitting on either side of him. Grant couldn't quite interpret any of the expressions.

As he focused on Secretary McKinley, the secretary responded, "Captain, this will be something considered by all parties. I'm scheduled to meet with the president once we're finished here. I know that isn't much, but it's all I can promise right now." He turned toward Simmons. "Ray, I'd like to bring the slides to the White House."

"Carl will ready them for you," Simmons responded, then said, "Captain, men, we all wish to thank you for giving us such accurate, honest details during this debriefing, and for your handling of the mission. So, unless there are more questions, by anyone, this meeting's over."

Grant immediately shook hands with his men. Words were unnecessary for any of them at the current moment.

McKinley stepped next to Grant, offered a hand, then asked, "Captain, will you be available tomorrow in case the president wishes details on the slides or other matters?"

"Of course, Mr. Secretary."

"All right."

Handshakes, and words of thanks continued as one by one everyone left.

*

The sun was just beginning to set when the men headed to their SUVs. They loosened their ties and un-buttoned their jackets, relieved that the debrief and the mission were over.

They got in the vehicles, except for Grant, who remained standing by the front passenger door, resting an arm on top of the door frame.

Adler was ready to start the engine, when he leaned over the console. "Well, where to? I hope dinner." Grant remained quiet. "Now what?" Adler said under his breath.

"I'll go check," Kalinin said, getting out of the rear seat. "Something bothering you, Grant?"

"What? Oh, Nick. I don't know. There are still unanswered questions."

"Such as?"

"The villagers."

"And Neman?"

"Yeah. And especially Neman."

"Nothing you can do, buddy," Kalinin said as he punched Grant's shoulder. "But what you can do is tell Joe where we're going for eats."

"You're right, Nick. That I can do. C'mon. And I'll call Scott. He deserves a night out, too."

A sharp, piercing whistle drew everyone's attention to five men running toward them. "Damn!" Grant said, waving.

"We didn't know if we'd catch you!" Salzman said offering his hand to Grant.

"Agent Salzman! It's great to see you, sir. It's great to see all of you." Grant shook Beatty's and Jacobs' hands. Though he didn't say anything, Grant noticed the still fresh scar on Jacobs' face. "Sirs, I'll let my men introduce themselves." While that happened, Grant turned toward two men who he hadn't yet met. "Sirs, are you Agents Nyland and Sands?"

"That we are, Captain," Nyland said offering his hand. "I'm Gary Nyland and this is Chuck Sands. It's good to be able to associate a voice with a face," Nyland laughed.

"Very true, sir. Listen, I'd like to say thanks for keeping the phone line open until you were ordered home."

"Sure. Listen, Chuck and I promised all of you drinks, but I understand those three guys did a one-up-manship and also offered dinner. So, we finally agreed to split it."

"Oh, sir, you don't have any idea on what and how much food my men can inhale! I'd like to chip in."

"Sorry. No way. C'mon. We've already got the restaurant picked out, right along the Potomac." Nyland whistled again. "We're outta here! Follow us."

As Grant got in the SUV, he thought, *Oh shit! I was gonna call Claudia.*

Adler started the engine. "Are we chipping in on the meal?"

"My offer was rejected."

"Well, now isn't that a damn shame! Let's go eat!"

Chapter 52

Tehran, Iran
Four Days After Mission

A small sign in red, white, and blue lettering was displayed above a table, celebrating the American Revolution Bicentennial. Warning signs were adhered to walls, cautioning that all power had to be turned off before opening machine covers. In other rooms, especially in soundproof rooms, there were teletype machines, coding-decoding equipment, radios, large size shredders, file cabinets, pictures of families. Everything had been left just as it was when the U.S. Embassy was overrun in 1979.

Leaving their offices on the second floor, Major General Behnam Khorasani and his Deputy Commander Brigadier General Mehdi Mokri, walked along the balcony, passing a continuous mural that covered entire walls on the first and second floors. Every scene, every building, every person depicted the takeover, along with references dating back to the U.S. in Vietnam.

But on this day both men ignored the mural they usually never failed to observe. For two days Khorasani had questioned all his officers during meetings, had reviewed a limited number of intercepted transmissions. All intel was thoroughly reviewed and researched.

He finally received three important reports: Colombian guerrillas, under the direction of his Quds Force, had made an attack on an operations building along a section of the pipeline. But neither the Colombians nor the Americans had responded to the demands, although, the Americans were unpredictable, especially when it pertained to hostages, and he assumed there were hostages.

The second report showed that the plane for Israel's Colombian ambassador had landed in Tel Aviv. Who was on-board was unknown. Such flights were not that unusual, but the timing seemed suspect.

And then, Colombian news agencies reported that Miguel Montoya had been arrested. Journalists speculated on everything from drugs, to espionage, to conspiracy. Khorasani decided that the arrest was the reason that everything had gone quiet. In every operation there is always a possibility that many things could go wrong. But the silence and lack of reports was still very troubling. *We should be celebrating a successful mission by now.*

He and Mokri walked through the open double doors leading outside. *There is the worry,* he thought, as he stood momentarily on the top step, looking toward the Southwest. How would the Israelis respond once they learned there were three dead Mossad agents?

Yet, there was one detail he was most anxious about —the disappearance of Tannaz Asadi. She was not on-board the *Al Sham* when it departed Buenaventura, nor were any of her teammates. *Perhaps they had taken refuge somewhere outside the city. Yes. That was possible after the attack on the operations building. The Colombians were most likely attempting to find the attackers. Asadi had orders to refrain from contacting us, but if she were in serious trouble, she had the means to make contact, and without detection.* A sick, nervous feeling began rising inside him.

His driver held open the rear door of the Citroën sedan. Mokri climbed in behind Khorasani, then both settled into the back seat. But Khorasani's mind was far from settled. He had been ordered to report to the office of Supreme Leader Hassan Esfahani to give a report on a mission that appeared to be faltering, if not already dead.

As the driver started the engine, one of Khorasani's officers rushed toward the vehicle, and tapped on the window. Khorasani rolled down the window, then took an envelope handed to him. Without responding, he signaled his driver to go. Ripping open the envelope, he read the new report, fixated on every word. His pulse quickened.

Mokri noticed the expression on Khorasani's face, but was unable to interpret whether it was anger, or dread. "What is wrong?!" He took the paper from Khorasani then read:

"News reports out of Colombia indicated government attacks had been made against guerrilla groups positioned at specific pump and block valve stations along the pipeline. The guerrillas were caught completely off guard. Many were injured or killed."

Without reading further, Mokri dropped the paper on the seat, now, more than ever, fearing the upcoming meeting with Supreme Leader Esfahani.

Silence prevailed during the remainder of the fifteen minute drive, but it was Khorasani whose mind reviewed every known incident in Colombia, trying to piece together some kind of report that would lessen the anger of the supreme leader, while knowing it was hopeless.

The successful attack on the operations building so far was the only high point. Was it possible Montoya had spilled his guts? He then thought about the arrival of the plane in Tel Aviv, the disappearance of . . . He grabbed the armrest. His knuckles turned white. *The plane! Could she have been . . .?*

At that instant an explosion shook the ground, blew out vehicle and building windows. A massive red-orange fireball consumed the Citroën. Doors blew open; the hood and trunk lid blew off. Thick, choking, black smoke rose into the air. Passersby and vehicles in the vicinity were struck by burning, razor-edged projectiles. Fire raged inside the Citroën, burning three, limbless bodies beyond recognition.

Two streets away and twelve minutes before the explosion, three men and two women waited for a bus. The men were dressed in typical garb: long sleeve white shirts, black pants, black jackets. The women wore loose-fitting blouses and slacks, lightweight long manteaus (overcoats) with colorful scarves covering their heads, wrapped loosely around their necks and shoulders.

A bus stopped, the women showed their tickets to the driver through the open door, then entered through the rear door. They took their seats, and placed plain, cloth shoulder bags on their laps. The men sat closer to the front, but separate from one another.

Everyone aboard the bus turned toward the sound, seeing black smoke rising above buildings. The driver kept light pressure on the gas pedal, then continued along the secondary road, only stopping when many of the shocked passengers demanded he let them off.

Nine passengers left the bus, all but five hurrying in different directions. The three men, with the two women following close by, continued walking one block further. Pedestrians ran past them, shouting and pointing toward the incident. Screams could be heard from blocks away.

They finally turned a corner, and headed to a parked van. The women got in the back, then quickly changed their outer wear to different color manteaus and scarves.

The vehicle pulled away slowly, while its driver and passengers noticed the traffic heading toward the explosion had come to a standstill. Drivers and passengers stared at the billowing smoke and fire.

Twenty-minutes later the van arrived at Mehrabad Airport, and continuing to use phony Iranian passports, the men purchased five round-trip tickets to Tabriz, Iran, although they had no intention of returning to Tehran. Within an hour, and after showing passports for a second time, they boarded the Iran Air flight.

Over the course of the remaining night hours, they would take two more flights, one to Ankara, Turkey, using another set of fake Iranian passports. For the final flight at 2230 hours, they switched to Israeli passports.

With their mission a success, five Mossad agents boarded a Turkish Airlines plane. Its destination—Tel-Aviv.

Epilogue

White House
Six Days After Mission
1445 Hours

Rachel, the president's office manager, walked toward Claudia Stockwell, who was filling out paperwork
for an upcoming White House event. Keeping her back
to the other women who were sitting at their desks,
Rachel said quietly, "You know that Captain Stevens will
be arriving soon for his three o'clock meeting
downstairs."

"Yes. We all have it on our calendars."

"Claudia, you and I have talked about the type of life
he led in the Navy and one that continues now. I've told
you I'd been through that same life with Craig, so I speak
from experience, and my heart. You're making a mistake
by walking out of his life. That's what you're doing, isn't
it?"

"How do you know that he isn't walking out of
mine?"

"Is he?" No response. "You've told me that he was a
good man in every sense of the word, besides being positively gorgeous."

Claudia finally looked up and smiled. "Yes, to both
comments. But it just won't work for me, Rachel. Not
that life anyway. And I would *never* ask him to give it
up."

"Well, then, I guess you've made up your mind."

"I guess so."

"I'm sorry to hear that." Leaning closer, then very quietly, and sadly, Rachel said, "You know, Claudia, men get broken hearts, too." She returned to her desk.

*

Situation Room
1455 Hours

Grant stood just outside the Sit Room, with his hands in his pockets, looking toward the stairs leading to the Oval Office. *Should I go see her after the meeting? Why bother? She already made her decision.*

He snapped his attention back to the upcoming meeting. The phone call from Rachel had instructed him to arrive at the West Gate entrance. The president and the upcoming meeting's attendees would join him in the Sit Room.

Saying he was anxious would be an understatement. He wondered, *Maybe there'll be more on Khorasani's sudden death by explosives. Will we finally learn Neman's fate? Did she even confess? Is she alive?* His thoughts were interrupted hearing the Oval Office door open.

President Carr led the others toward the Sit Room. He smiled and extended a hand to Grant. "Welcome home, Grant."

"Thank you, Mr. President."

"Gentlemen," Carr said, leading everyone into the room. The meetings' participants took their seats.

Grant glanced at each man: Vice President Forbes,

Secretary of State McKinley, Directors Simmons and Franklin, Secretary of Defense Daniels. *Not a big party,* he thought.

Carr stood by the table, laying down a folder. "Gentlemen, early this morning the Israeli ambassador delivered an envelope. Directors Simmons and Franklin have already reviewed its contents." Carr nodded toward someone standing near the Watch Room, who turned on an overhead projector. "This, gentlemen," Carr said, "is a partial transcript of the Israeli's report on Ashira Neman."

On the pull down screen the typed report appeared:

TOP SECRET

ASHIRA NEMAN
A.K.A. TANNAZ ASADI

Re: Ashira Neman; birth name, Tannaz Asadi - Born in District Four, Tehran, Iran

Father: Pejman Asadi, Lieutenant Colonel in Iranian Army; a.k.a. Eli Hassid

Mother: Laleh Alinejad

Brother: Kayree Asadi

Lieutenant Colonel Pejman Asadi had volunteered to act as a spy for Iran. After two years in Israel, he was captured near the heavy-water nuclear reactor facility in

315

the Negev Desert, twenty-five miles Southwest of the Dead Sea. His passport and papers showed an Israeli name of "Eli Hassid" but these proved to be fake. Under interrogation he admitted that he attempted to gather intelligence on whether the facility was being used to produce nuclear materials that could lead to the production of nuclear weapons. The Israelis sentenced him to life in prison at the maximum security penitentiary in Ramla. He was shot and killed during an attempted escape, his body never returned to Iran.

Pejman Asadi had left his family behind in Iran, telling them he was being temporarily assigned. But days before his departure, Tannaz accidentally found his fake Israeli passport. In order to protect herself and her family, she was wise enough to understand that that knowledge had to remain with her forever.

While he was gone, her mother would tell her stories about the difficulties women had before the Pahlavi Regime came to power. Many times Tannaz would hear from her mother how lucky Iranian women were to gain more freedom under his regime.

But for her, just gaining some freedom was not enough. Secretly, she wanted to learn all she could about the Iranian military. She specifically chose her uncle to learn from, since he was a major general in the Iranian Army. Her brother, who was eight years older than she, and who had lost a leg fighting during the Omani Civil War, was her confidant and source of information. There were times, though, that he warned her about her curiosity, but she persisted.

Although she was not yet a teenager, she had already

devised a way to eventually serve her country, and to somehow learn the truth about her father. It would take intelligence and patience, but she would find a way.

Her uncle began to realize that one day she could become a valuable asset for Iran. While there was no possibility of women joining the Iranian military, Israel did accept its women into its IDF, and its elite Mossad. He presented his idea to higher authorities. It had taken months before his idea was finally approved. Tannaz was immediately and secretly schooled in the Hebrew language and all things Israeli.

Years later, Tannaz Asadi left Iran, with a new passport, new papers, and a new name. Through channels arranged by her uncle and government, she entered Israel not as an immigrant, but as a legal citizen. Her new life had just begun. She served in the IDF, excelling in every skill during training, which would bring her the attention she needed to eventually be selected for Mossad.

Already thinking and planning ahead, she secretly created a code word to use on her first mission, from the name her father had on his fake Israeli passport: Hassid stood for "Righteous."

*

The screen went blank, and lights were turned on. Carr spoke, "As I said, that's only a partial report. The remainder of it showed issues and events that had been verified and resolved by parties in this room."

"Excuse me, sir," Grant said, "there were reports from several years back on Shahbaz. How . . .?"

Simmons cut in, "Iranian disinformation, Captain. They were dishing it out, making us chase our tails, hoping that when she began her first mission we'd doubt our own intel."

"They succeeded," Grant grumbled.

"Indeed they did," Simmons said. "As an FYI, there was a separate interrogation report from her teammate, Piruz Zare, confirming the plan for taking over the pipeline. We thought you'd be most interested in her background, though."

"It helped, sir. Will I have permission to reveal any of this to my men?"

"Of course."

"Sir, is it safe to say that the dead Mossad agents' bodies have been returned to Israel?"

"They have, along with the four live Iranians, who are being held somewhere in Tel Aviv. I think we should leave it at that."

"Of course, sir. This will be my last question, because you won't be able to answer what would've been my second question. Is she still alive?"

Simmons drummed his fingers on the table, while keeping his eyes on Grant. "Yes, she is. I would think, eventually, you'll find out the answer to that second question, Captain, which was probably where she's being held."

"That was it, sir," Grant smiled.

Simmons glanced down at a paper. "One other item you'll probably be interested in, is the Colombian's boarded the *Al Sham* just before she departed Buenaventura. They arrested a dozen men who belonged to the local guerrilla organization. We're waiting for updates."

"Good to hear, sir. Guess the Colombians finally got some backbone, sir."

"Uh, yes, it would appear so."

"Grant, do you have anything else to offer, or have questions?" Carr asked.

"I don't believe so, sir. I appreciate the intel."

"Any questions from anyone for Grant?" Shaking of heads was everyone's answer. "All right then. Grant, we have another meeting on a different matter. So, we'll turn you loose."

"Thank you, sirs." Grant rolled his chair back.

"And Grant," Carr said, standing and extending his hand, "congratulations on a successful mission."

Grant returned Carr's firm grip. "Thank you, Mr. President. I'll pass that along to my men, sir."

Five minutes later, Grant was in his Vette, talking on the phone with Adler. "Joe, I'm just leaving the 'House.'"

"How'd it go?"

"Not as much info as I'd hoped for, but I've been given permission to pass along the little I did learn. Listen, I've got a few hours before picking up Luke at the airport. Why don't you touch base with the guys and Scott, and have them meet at my apartment? I'll pick up dinner."

"Sounds like a plan. Uh, I don't know if you'll wanna answer this, but did you see Claudia?"

"To answer simply, Joe, the matter was best left alone."

"Are you all right?"

"Sure."

"Okay. See ya soon."

Grant drove from the parking area, thinking, *It's time to clear your brain and move on, Stevens. You're gonna be with your son in a few hours.*

*

Tel Aviv, Israel
0100 Hours - Local Time

A nondescript, dark gray panel van backed up to a side entry. All building and vehicle lights were off. A hooded, handcuffed prisoner was led from the building by two security men. The prisoner was assisted into the cargo bed, seated, then secured. Doors closed quietly. Within seconds the vehicle was driven from Mossad headquarters, with its destination forty-five miles north, and five miles west of Atlit, a city on the coast.

At 0150 the van stopped at a security gate. Papers were handed to one of the heavily armed guards, who inspected the cargo bed, before waving the driver through.

Inside the cargo bed, Ashira Neman/Tannaz Asadi was wondering whether her government or her family knew she was alive, or whether there would be negotiations for her release. Somehow, she felt that would not even be considered, by either country. Her greatest, most emotional regret was never discovering what really happened to her father. Israel announced a spy had been killed escaping, but she never believed it to be the truth. Even as Mossad, the details available to her still left unanswered questions.

The van stopped, the engine shut down, the doors opened. She was led from the vehicle, and onto the grounds of Prison Six, officially Confinement Base 396, an Israeli military prison. This is where she would begin serving her twenty-five year sentence in solitary confinement. This was her fate.

GRANT AND HIS MEN WILL RETURN! KEEP
AN EYE OUT FOR #18 BY FOLLOWING MY
BLOG:
JFREDRIC.BLOGSPOT.COM

Acknowledgements

Navy SEALs, all SpecOps, Active Service Members: - Thank you for your service, sacrifice, and dedication in keeping America safe, and protecting everyone, anywhere, anytime. You make us proud!

To All Veterans: We thank you for your service and sacrifice. You will always be remembered.

Witchdoctor 7 - Welcome back to the world! Welcome home!! Thanks for being willing to 'jump' right back in and share your special knowledge.

K. Ford - Very much appreciated all your time, ideas, and editing assistance -- with a few laughs thrown in along the way. Thank you!

And thanks to all Grant Stevens' fans for your continuing support. Hooyah!

Printed in Poland
by Amazon Fulfillment
Poland Sp. z o.o., Wrocław

49076180R00181